Bleak Winds of Destiny

The Rebel Raiders are heading for New Mexico territory to rob the bank in Tucumcari. Major Deke Hogan, a Civil War guerrilla fighter, heads the contingent. The proceeds of the attack are intended to support the Confederacy in a last ditch effort to regain the initiative. But destiny has played a mean trick when Hogan discovers that the surrender had been signed by General Lee three weeks previously.

From being a legitimate fighting force, the Raiders have become nothing more than common outlaws. Their escape does not pass unchallenged. And further trouble erupts between surviving gang members as to how the loot should be distributed. Hogan wants to use it for the regeneration of the decimated South, whereas a hot-headed tearaway called Dusty Blue figures they should split the take among themselves.

What happens when tempers flare and bullets fly could never have been foreseen by any of them.

Bleak Winds of Destiny

Dale Graham

A Black Horse Western

ROBERT HALE

© Dale Graham 2019
First published in Great Britain 2019

ISBN 978-0-7198-2884-3

The Crowood Press
The Stable Block
Crowood Lane
Ramsbury
Marlborough
Wiltshire SN8 2HR

www.bhwesterns.com

Robert Hale is an imprint
of The Crowood Press

The right of Dale Graham to be identified as
author of this work has been asserted by him
in accordance with the Copyright, Designs and
Patents Act 1988

ONE

BORDER CROSSING

A powerful wind was blowing off the arid Prairie Dog flats as the line of riders crossed the border into New Mexico: five weary men huddled down and caked in dust, heads bowed beneath wide-brimmed hats pulled low for protection against the harsh particles of sand. Five weathered faces, pinched and drawn from too little sleep, feeling old before their time.

They had been on the trail constantly for four days without let-up, and the strain was showing. Even the youngest of the party, a sharp-shooting sniper called Dusty Blue, was wilting under the hot blast of the sandstorm.

The leader gave a sigh of relief as they passed the weather-beaten signboard. A scowl, however, cloaked his craggy features on reading a second missive pinned beneath by some mocking comedian that read *Johnny Rebs cross here at your peril.* An ominous precursor of what was to follow.

Major Deke Hogan shrugged off the threat. He was somewhere between the age of thirty and fifty – it was hard to tell at this stage of the brutal Civil War, now in its fourth year. A craggy-faced veteran, he had risen through the ranks due to his tenacity and determination, dogged attributes that had brought him to the notice of General Lee himself after saving the commander's life at Cold Harbour. And like their allegiance to Lee, Hogan's men were equally willing to follow him into the very jaws of death.

None of the men were in uniform, including Hogan who was in charge of this contingent of Confederate guerrillas known as the Rebel Raiders. When he had first suggested the idea of a small force able to strike quick and disappear even quicker, General Lee had been the most ardent supporter of the enterprise. 'Make sure you grab as much dough as possible from them Union banks, men,' he had endorsed with avid enthusiasm. 'We need every last dollar to carry the fight back to the North.'

Numerous other splinter groups had likewise been authorized to hammer the enemy within their own sphere of operations. William Clarke Quantrill was the most renowned. But Major Hogan and his hand-picked gang had proved to be as adept as any at securing those essential funds with the least need for brutal tactics.

Hogan's meeting with the renowned Confederate general had been six months before. His force had since wreaked havoc amidst the Union enclaves, earning them the dubious reputation of being ruthless predators acknowledged far and wide through their rebellious nickname. The men had revelled in their notoriety.

Unlike the more infamous Bloody Bill Anderson, who hungrily lived up to his grizzly sobriquet, Deke Hogan was an adherent of non-violent methods. Killings there had been, but only in self-defence or if an attack on the enemy forces presented itself. Civilians were deemed to be non-active participants, and any man who deliberately stepped over the line was swiftly dealt with. One member of the group who had later bragged about burning down a homestead after murdering the occupants for disputing the acquisition of fresh horses, was summarily hanged. A harsh lesson from Major Hogan, but essential, in his opinion, to maintain the integrity of the Confederate cause.

That said, in recent days rumblings of discontent had been emerging about the need for a break from hostilities. It was a legitimate claim. And Hogan had agreed that following this next job, they would head back to friendly territory for some much needed rest and relaxation.

Crossing the border into New Mexico meant they were getting close to this final clash. Tucumcari was only a day's ride to the west. Intelligence gained from a dependable source had indicated the bank there was holding upwards of twenty thousand dollars in greenbacks. It was alleged to be back pay for blue belly troopers stationed in nearby Forts Union,

Bascom and Sumner. The Raiders intended to divert every last dollar to the Southern cause.

'I sure am glad to see the back of Texas, and no mistake,' Hogan muttered over his shoulder to the man behind.

All he received back from his second-in-command, a tough wiry jigger sporting a shock of red hair called Blaze Pender, was a muttered grunt. Trapped inside the howling mayhem, none of the others even heard their leader's remark. Heads were bent forward to deflect the harsh sand blasting. They were all thinking of their own back pay and how much liquor and girls it would buy.

But the threat of danger was ever present. Only the previous day they had been caught in the open by a Union patrol and forced to flee for their lives. It was fortunate that their horses were well rested, unlike the blue belly mounts, enabling them to escape without any casualties. Crossing the border into a new territory was a distinct relief. Most enemy patrols tended to stick with their own patch, but such adherence to border legislation had no meaning for guerrilla bands such as the Raiders.

Hogan pulled his hat further down. The sandstorm had been raging all day – though at least in this murk they would be safe from any wandering patrols, themselves lost in the swirling sand clouds. Bringing up the rear was Rib-eye Charlie Bone, the oldest member of the contingent – and in Hogan's view the steadiest and most unflappable. Rib-eye could always be relied on to keep that lone peeper open for trouble, be it of natural or human origin. He had lost the other eye to a piece of cannon shrapnel at Chancellorsville.

An hour later, Hogan called a halt in the shelter of a rocky overhang. Dark shadows infiltrating the hazy murk meant sundown was not far off. 'We'll rest up here for the night, boys,' Hogan declared, much to the relief of all concerned. 'Get a fire going,' he ordered a scowling Dusty Blue. The yellow-haired kid always moaned when it was his turn for preparing the chow. Hogan knew it was best ignored. 'The rest of you see to your own horses, then make sure all your weapons are clean and ready for action. We'll hit the Tucumcari bank tomorrow at opening time.'

Hogan himself sat on a rock musing over how best to lift that dough without having to fall back on any gunplay. He was later joined by Pender. 'You been to this place before, Major?' he enquired of the thoughtful officer.

Hogan shook his head. 'All I know is what Captain Travers told me back in Plainview. The bank in Tucumcari is holding Union army backpay, which needs to be lifted before the end of the month.' He removed a well worn pocket book from his sheepskin coat and thumbed the pages. 'That means we've only gotten another three days before the local bluecoats arrive to collect it.'

'Not much time left then,' remarked Pender, stroking his stubble-coated chin. 'All on account of that danged patrol that forced us to make a detour.'

'And don't be forgetting the storm, old buddy,'

interrupted Hogan. 'We gotta pray that it's blown off by the morning.' On all sides of the welcome shelter, the howling gale continued its relentlessly savage onslaught.

'Reckon the gods were on our side when we found this refuge,' Pender remarked watching the billowing sand hammering by overhead. He was hungry and looking forward to whatever Dusty Blue served up.

Hogan nodded, though his mind was focused on how best to lift the dough. 'The South badly needs that money,' he added in a measured tone. 'It could give Lee the edge to turn the tide in our favour.'

The two old pals had been together through thick and thin during the whole conflict, having signed up after the first shots were fired at Fort Sumter back in April of 1861. A tense silence gripped them as thoughts harked back to battles won and lost – though more of the latter in recent times. Both knew that the Confederacy was being pushed back on all fronts, but they still held the view that General Lee was the better strategist. It was up to individual forces like theirs to deliver the wherewithal to effect a spirited revival.

It was Hogan who broke in on their mutual cogitations. 'We'll need to recce the place first, get the lie of the land and work out a suitable escape route.' Ever the optimist, Deke Hogan still had faith that victory for the South could be achieved. The others appeared to harbour similar expectations. And it was this positive attitude that had made them such a successful undercover fighting unit.

They both looked up as a stocky jasper called Banjo Brakewell began picking out the notes of Yankee Doodle. Rib-eye joined him on harmonica. It was a regular occurrence when they made camp, and was encouraged by Hogan to keep up morale. Even Blue hummed along while busying himself getting the usual chow ready – though refried beans with bacon and cornbread were becoming a mite tiresome. Old Rib-eye was dreaming of the succulent steaks that accompanied his nickname, and he wasn't the only one.

'Be good to rest up a-while,' the officer ruminated dreamily, accepting a plate of the unwholesome fare with a grateful smile, 'Not to mention some decent grub for a change!' – although he made sure that Blue was out of earshot. Following some desultory chitchat around the fire, they settled down for the night. With the hard ground for a mattress and sleeping under a blanket of flying sand, a few nights in a soft warm bed could not come soon enough for them all.

TWO

ASHES TO
ASHES. . . .

The next morning they were up at first light, awakened by Charlie Bone's crudely delivered hollers. Grumbling complaints informed the human rooster where to stick his toothless evocations. Bone was always up first, appearing to have a built-in alarm system. He was followed by Hogan, who issued a sigh of relief from between gritted teeth. His prayer had been answered. The storm had passed on, revealing a scintillating backdrop in the east, a host of colours splashed across the dawn canvas.

Breakfast was a hurried affair of beef jerky and hot coffee to wake them up. They were soon on the trail, just as the new day's corona was peeping above the notched skyline of the Palo Duro range to their rear. Good progress was made across the rolling plains of bunch grass and blue stem.

12

Blunt outcroppings worn down into isolated flat-topped mesas lay dotted across the featureless terrain, like islands in a dull ochre sea. The most prominent of these was their destination, a noble upthrust of grey rock capped with a black headdress rising majestically out of the early morning haze. Tucumcari Mountain stood hauntingly forbidding over the town that had adopted its name – and no wonder, in view of its tragic history.

An old Apache legend handed down through the years tells of a chief who lived there with his beautiful daughter, Kari. Two braves were chosen as prospective husbands – Tocom whom she loved, and Tonapon, a surly roughneck no young bride would ever choose. The chief suggested a duel with daggers to decide who would win her hand in marriage. When Tonopan slew his rival, Kari ran out from hiding and killed him with her own knife before she herself fell on the weapon. On hearing the awful news, the chief also killed himself crying out 'Tocom-Kari' in a mournful wail.

The name had stuck, and Tucumcari had grown into a major supply centre for the Union forces in the area. Hogan and his men approached the settlement by means of a low ridge to the south. Here he signalled a halt, using a pair of binoculars to scrutinize the lie of the land from the lofty perch.

Four streets met at a central plaza surrounded by trees with a well in the middle. Nobody was yet abroad. Beyond the confines of the town, trails radiated outwards to the four points of the compass. A careful study revealed a single brick-built structure on the west side of the plaza, which, according to his experience, was likely to be the bank. Of the trails on offer, that to the north seemed the best prospect of evading capture. Broken mesa country beyond Tucumcari Mountain would allow them to vanish in the labyrinth of canyons.

And No Man's Land was only a couple of day's hard ride away. With no legal jurisdiction yet established within the narrow Panhandle sandwiched between Colorado and Texas, the Raiders could rest up there without fear of reprisal. All they needed to watch out for were outlaw bands with no allegiance to anybody but themselves, since any hint of the twenty thousand bucks would be an irresistible attraction to villains like bees to a honey pot.

Hogan hooked out a pocket watch and flipped open the lid. A melodic chorus tinkled merrily, totally at odds with the tension gripping the watching Raiders. Every hit produced the same hollow feeling in the pit of the stomach. They were never the same, some more tricky than others with no certainty of easy pickings. Yet each man had sworn an oath of allegiance, dedicating his whole being in support of the Confederacy. Hogan glanced along the line, satisfied they were as ready as they would ever be for the upcoming action.

'Usual procedure, boys,' he declared. 'We go in slow and ride out fast. This time it's Rib-eye and Banjo to hold the horses and keep watch.' For each raid, apart from himself, Hogan rotated his men. On this occasion Dusty Blue and Blaze Pender would partner him for the actual heist. A reproving eye fastened on to the hot headed Blue. 'And this time, Dusty, keep that hogleg under control. There weren't no need to crack that bank manager over the head in Amarillo.'

Blue scowled. 'He ought not to have said them things about us fellas being slave whippers. My folks don't hold with that side of things. Never have done.'

Much as Hogan sympathized with the kid's view, they were soldiers engaged in a military conflict where only those fighting for the opposing side were considered fair game when it came to violence – and only then with action agreed in the Rules of War signed by the respective leaders. 'You know the score, kid. Make sure you toe the line. I don't want any loose cannons in my detachment.' Maintaining a deadpan look, stony yet indomitable, Deke Hogan waited for a response.

Blue held his caustic glower for a moment before looking away. 'Sure thing, Major. Just saying, is all. You can count on me.'

A palpable relaxation settled over the others. They had all expressed reservations in private regarding the kid's reliability.

'OK boys, then let's ride,' Hogan announced. 'We got us a bank to rob.'

Descending a meandering narrow deer track in single file, Major Hogan led the way, passing through a stand of pine trees. Jack rabbits and chirpy chipmunks scurried out of their way, ogling these alien intruders with dismay. Tension gripped the men as they neared the town: according to their leader it prevented a careless attitude and kept them alert.

When they reached the edge of the town, the usual procedure was adopted. It was a successful ploy that had stood them in good stead on previous forays into unknown settlements. Hogan and the two men allocated to enter the bank walked their horses along the middle of the southbound trail separate from the others so as to avoid any unnecessary attention.

The back-ups entered Tucumcari by a different route. Their arrival was timed to arrive at the bank just after their buddies had entered. Searching eyes probed the streets seeking out any unknown variable that might upset the apple cart.

Few people were abroad at that time in the morning. Early risers, mainly cowhands and farmers, were already out of town engaged in their daily labours. A few storekeepers were sweeping their stoops. None gave the newcomers more than a cursory glance, which was just as it should be. Hogan smiled to himself as he nudged the grey mare over to a hitching rail outside a tobacconist's adjacent to the bank. A sign creaked on rusty hinges as the three men casually dismounted. Effecting a casual manner was second nature to these men – yet still they felt on edge.

The bank's blinds had just been raised. A thought flitted through the officer's mind as to how these places always seemed to adopt the same format. It had made their task all the easier in the past, and there was no reason to suppose Tucumcari would be any different. They stepped up on to the boardwalk, had a last look round, then along to the bank. Only now were guns drawn and cocked.

A pause, a drawing-in of breath, and they hustled inside. The edginess of the initial groundwork was displaced as concentration bonded with excitement. The thrill of facing danger now took command. They were soldiers engaged in combat against a formidable enemy. Two cashiers were behind the counter, with a third, the manager, seated behind a large desk over to one side. They might be civilians, but any lapse of single-mindedness could find these jaspers fighting back.

'Keep your hands in the air, and don't make any stupid moves,' Hogan snapped out crisply, pointing his Army Remington .44 at the manager. Pender and Blue aimed menacing snarls at the two cashiers. Both employees were open mouthed and clearly terrified by this violent intrusion into their mundane daily lives. 'This is a hold-up on behalf of the Confederate States of America. Now empty that safe and fill this sack.' He tossed the bag on to the manager's desk. 'Leave the loose cash. All we want are the greenbacks.'

Blue's eyes glazed over at all that dough he could see stacked in the open safe behind the manager's desk. It was always the same when they robbed a bank. Yet all the dough, apart from a mediocre payment allotted by the government, was bound for the Southern capital in Richmond, Virginia. More

17

and more of late, the kid had started to question why they couldn't have a bigger share of the payout – after all, weren't they doing all the hard work? So far he had only voiced these concerns to his pal Banjo Brakewell.

The bank manager froze, staring down the barrel of the threatening revolver. His beady eyes popped behind the round spectacles. The bald-headed coot was unable to comprehend what was happening. 'Shift your ass, mister!' Hogan rasped, waving his gun in front of the rotund kisser. 'We ain't got all day. This dough is needed for a better cause than drinking money for those damned blue bellies.'

That was when the manager found his voice. 'B-but the w-war is over,' he stuttered out. 'Lee signed the surrender at Appomatox three weeks ago.'

'That's a darned lie,' Pender exclaimed. 'We'd have heard about it. Now get over to that safe and fill the sack.'

Although equally sceptical, Hogan was more circumspect. 'You ain't trying to trick us, are you?' he snapped, injecting an intimidating threat into his query. 'That would be mighty foolish.' The gun jerked forward.

'Honest, mister,' the banker pleaded, sweat dribbling down his ruddy cheeks. 'We got the news last week from the stagecoach driver. And it was in the *Clovis Tribune* as well. The war's over.'

This sudden announcement had caught the three robbers on the wrong foot. One of the tellers, a young cockspur who had been under age to join the

Union army, now saw his chance to achieve some notoriety among his pals. His hand slipped under the counter searching for the small Beals pocket pistol kept for just such an emergency as this. Thus far it had never been used in anger. Foiling a gang of ruthless bank robbers would be a feather in his cap with the girls, too.

Anxiety gripped the youngster as he took hold of the gun. But this nervous flicker in his demeanour was a dead giveaway to a hardened guerrilla fighter like Dusty Blue. Barely more than a couple of years senior to the teller, he read the signs like a veteran, and his own gun swung, blasting a hole in the teller's chest the size of a bunched fist.

The deafening explosion was followed by a second shot to ensure the danger was truly nullified. Time stood still for a brief flicker as the shock of death tightened its icy grip. 'I didn't have any choice,' Blue declared, striving to justify his action. 'The darned fool was trying to make a name for himself by pulling a gun.'

Suddenly the whole rationale of the freedom fighters and its justification was altered. And all it had taken was for one brash idiot to overturn their *modus operandi*. This abrupt twist of fortune stunned the three Raiders. Hogan was the first to recover his wits. No sense in berating the junior member of his team. The military unit had now turned from guerrilla fighters into nought but murdering bank robbers. There was no escaping that unwholesome fact, so they might as well continue with the planned task.

Without considering the implications, he punched out his orders. 'You two grab the dough quick. Lee might have surrendered, but the Rebel Raiders are still in business.'

Hogan kept a close watch on the two cowering bank employees while Blue and Pender grabbed the cash haul. 'Quick as you can, boys. Those shots will have been heard.' Even as he uttered the fateful warning, gunfire erupted outside in the plaza. 'Time we were out of here,' he exhorted pulling open the front door.

Dusty Blue was the first out. Ducking low he managed to avoid a rash of shots plucking slivers of wood from the door post. His own pistol reply struck a man careless enough to be standing out in the open. The victim went down, encouraging the other citizens to take cover. Pender was not so fortunate. He was shot in the leg. The sack of money fell from his hand. 'Mount up, Blaze,' Hogan called from behind. 'I've gotten the dough.'

Dragging the shattered leg behind him like a heavy log, Blaze Pender struggled to heave himself up into the saddle. Blood was pouring from the smashed kneecap. The injury made him a sitting target for irate townsfolk eager to prevent this violation of their peaceful settlement.

For four years the war had somehow passed them by. Now over, it was a brutal twist of fate to have struck the town. Nobody as yet was aware of these unlucky ramifications: to the citizens of Tucumcari this was a straightforward bank robbery. And they had no intentions of succumbing without firm retaliation.

A half dozen slugs punctured Pender's body. Lifeless as a sack of coal, the war veteran's life was terminated in the most ill-omened of circumstances. Cheers erupted from the galvanized townsmen, encouraging others to join the fray in making a determined stand.

Brakewell was the next to go down. The banjo strapped to his saddle disintegrated in a jangling cacophony of snapped strings before the player himself was toppled from his horse. Dogs joined in the hullaballoo, adding to the mayhem. Hogan knew that the end was nigh for the three survivors unless they grabbed the initiative.

'Remember Topeka, boys!' he shouted out. 'Mount up and let's give 'em hell on the hoof!' The occasion to which he was referring had occurred four months previously and had involved a similar retaliation. All guns blazing, they had ridden straight at the enemy scattering them like chaff in the wind.

'Yahooooooo!' Bone replied hollering like some demented banshee. 'We're with you, Major.' The exuberant rallying cry was cut short by a stray bullet hacking a chunk out of his ear. Not enough to stall his flight, it had drawn blood, encouraging the crowd to rush at these marauding desperadoes.

Riding three abreast, the surviving Raiders responded by charging straight at the milling throng. With a pistol in each hand while gripping the reins between clenched teeth, hot lead was pumped out.

Neither Dusty Blue nor Charlie Bone gave any thought to what they might hit. Escape was now the main issue.

Only Deke Hogan aimed high, not wishing to worsen the dire situation into which they had been pitched. He still could barely credit that General Lee had gone back on his determination to fight on. Had things deteriorated so much since their last meeting? Clearly the answer was a resounding yes! And he couldn't help feeling let down, betrayed even, by the man he had so revered. All that dough from previous raids ploughed back into the Southern cause was now a daydream, a flight of fantasy.

A sharp barb of pain lanced through his left arm, bringing his reflections back to their current predicament. A loose bullet had plucked at his sleeve. Head down, he urged his remaining men onwards, the sack of money still in evidence slung over the saddle horn. At least they had something to retrieve from this catastrophe. But there was still the serious business of getting out of the town.

It was a bold move intended to strike fear into the shambolic mob, a desperate ploy from men used to living on their wits. But unlike their opponents, they were prepared to take chances by working together as a team. And it worked. Unprepared for such bald-faced retaliation, the crowd were brushed aside easily, enabling the fugitives to burst out of the plaza.

Some desultory firing pursued them, but the fiery reaction to the robbery had lost its heat. The Raiders were soon able to disappear along the northern trail heading for Tucumcari Mountain at a fast clip. The canyonlands beyond offered a variety of twisting routes through which pursuit would be well nigh impossible.

Only when they had left the flat plains behind and were climbing across the lower flanks of the mountain did Hogan call a halt in a copse of Joshua trees. From their elevated position, it was clear to see that no pursuit had as yet been organized. With at least two townsfolk dead and numerous injuries to treat, immediate concerns would be elsewhere. After all was said and done, the stolen money was the army's responsibility, not that of the Tucumcari town council.

A wry smile broke across Hogan's face. But there was no escaping the grim fact that now presented itself. The once justifiable havoc wrought under the banner of military law by the infamous Rebel Raiders had now degenerated into nothing more than lawless skulduggery. In the eyes of a post-war society administered by Abe Lincoln's Northern Union, they were nothing but anarchist renegades, their only reward for four years of brutal conflict being the hangman's noose.

'So what we gonna do with this dough, Major?' Rib-eye expostulated that night after they had made camp in a secluded draw. Ever since their getaway, the older man had been mulling over the implications of the heist and its unfortunate aftermath.

THREE

. . . DUST TO DUST

Bone was not the only one harbouring thoughts concerning the fate of the stolen payroll. Blue likewise was eager to hear what their leader had in mind – although in his case a greed-induced stare kept shifting towards that heavy sack packed full of dough. None of that worthless Confederate rubbish, these were legitimate banknotes. 'I can't wait to get my share,' he announced, a lovely feeling of elation swirling around inside. 'Then it'll be spend, spend, spend!'

The kid's own thoughts were clearly hankering after all the girls and booze his cut of the proceeds would buy. Now the war was over, Blue had taken it as a done deal that the money was theirs. And with only three of them left, the share-out would be substantial. His rapacious eyes glittered in the firelight, a leery smile already spreading across his face at the thought of those lovely greenbacks.

The three survivors were sat round the camp fire drinking coffee and chewing on the stringy meat from a jack rabbit potted by Bone with his trusty .40 calibre Remington Rolling Block. The weapon had never been known to leave his side, even when asleep.

Deke Hogan tossed the leg bone into the fire, the grease sizzling just like his own thoughts as he contemplated the vital question Rib-eye Charlie had posed. He had not failed to heed the covetous looks that the young hothead made no attempt to hide. Initially, the officer's view had roamed along similar lines. Why not keep the money? After all, didn't they deserve a substantial reward for all the support they had given to the Confederacy over the last few years?

But that would make him nothing but a common thief, an outlaw on the run with honest men's blood on his hands and all others turned against him. Deke Hogan had always liked to think of himself as a latterday Robin Hood-type figure – a gallant hero riding alongside his merry men who only robbed in order to further the cause to which he was aligned.

Now freed from the yoke of military discipline, did he really want to toss that aside like a discarded old shirt? Other guerrilla fighters in his line of work had fostered similar intentions to pass on their ill-gotten gains to those who needed it most. Top of the list were the James boys and their cousins the Youngers who would soon be riding the owlhooter trail, having abandoned such high ideals.

Hogan stood up and sauntered across to the edge of the flickering firelight. Puffing hard on a cheroot, he broodingly sifted through the options available. One-third of twenty big ones would set him up for life, some place beyond the frontier where he could settle down, buy some land and maybe take a wife to help him run it.

All very enticing. But then his conscience began to make its presence felt. Not the guilt associated with the robbery itself. But men had been killed, which made him a murderer by association. Robin Hood broke the law, but only to serve the greater good of his country. Deke Hogan would follow a similar path. Suddenly, the mist cleared and he knew straightaway which trail to follow.

Top of the list were the holdings back in Missouri where his folks and other relations had been badly affected by the brutal conflict. Too many innocent people had suffered in the past four years. And they were going to need all the help they could secure to rebuild shattered lives. Only when the money had been fairly distributed could he head west to make a fresh start, in lands where the Rebel Raiders' reputation would count for nothing, a distant memory buried forever.

'Come on, Hogan,' Blue rasped, suspecting the direction in which his old superior's thoughts were heading. It was a curt demand. Gone was the subservient tone of the day before. 'When are we gonna get our share of the loot?'

The surly manner spoke volumes that the kid had

no intention of adopting a benevolent approach to the allocation of their illicit haul. Such an assumption would need to be squashed before trouble erupted. Hogan turned to face his two partners in crime. Straightaway he made his views known, still imbuing the decision in crisp military parlance.

'Soon as the heat dies down, we'll head back east and make sure this dough goes to benefit the South.' Negative looks from both men were enough to indicate his intentions were not being reciprocated. Rib-eye's hangdog disappointment was less bluntly publicized than Blue's overt display of hostility. Hogan nonetheless pressed on, softening the unwelcome receipt of his aim with what he considered a just reward. 'You boys will be paid the going rate for your services to the Cause with the addition of a two hundred dollar bonus apiece.' A positive smile declared his accepted notion that this was a fair outcome.

Not as far as Dusty Blue was concerned. Not by a long chalk. The kid's whole body stiffened assuming a threatening pose. 'Ease off, kid,' Bone urged, laying a restraining hand on the young tearaway's arm. 'That don't seem such a bad deal the Major is proposing. And we all want what's best for our kinfolks back home. Yeah?'

The mealy-mouthed response elicited a scornful grunt from Blue. 'It's an insult to all we've been through. Busting our guts for a Cause that's been blown apart. I say we keep the dough. We darned well earned it, and more.' The snarled expletive was followed up with mocking derision. 'And don't be calling this guy "Major" any more. His authority ended with that lily-livered surrender. Three darned weeks since. He's just one of us now.'

Hogan slowly stood up and faced the blustering youth. 'You want that money, Blue, it's over yonder. But you'll have to go through me to get it.' He hunkered down, rugged face set in stone, right hand hovering above the holstered Army Remington on his hip.

A rabid snarl hissed from between gritted teeth as Blue flexed his own right hand. 'I been wondering for some time if'n you're as quick on the draw as you'd have us believe.' Bone stepped back out the line of fire. This had gone past the point of no return. Nothing he could say would stop the reckless Blue Eyes from finding out the truth for himself.

'Well, now's your chance to find out,' Hogan replied, his whole attention focusing on the slight twitch in the kid's left eye. 'It's your call.' He had spotted the tell-tale sign of an imminent draw when a Union army sergeant had recognized Blue back in Sedalia. Time had hung heavy as both men girded themselves for the age-old challenge to be played out to its terminal finale. The trooper had gone down.

Blue was equally confident that a showdown with Deke Hogan would produce the same result. Thin lines prowled out from the twitching thin lips, ageing the kid far more than his twenty-three years. His eyes were laughing but no humour reached the sneering grin as he grabbed for his pistol, clearing leather

28

with slick dexterity. The gun barrel rose, a thumb drawing back the hammer.

The momentary signal, fractions of a second prior to the kid's draw, found Hogan responding. So fast was his reflex action that the watching Bone missed it. The Remington spat forth its lethal charge, smashing Blue's gun and removing his little finger.

The kid cried out in shock more than pain. That would come later. He staggered back, tumbling over his saddle. The blood had drained from his youthful face as the notion registered that he had been bested, but was still very much alive. The winner's smoking six-gun shifted to cover Bone, who was equally mesmerized by the sudden outbreak of violence and its unexpected outcome.

'Better see to him, Charlie,' Hogan said, gesturing for the older man to staunch the bleeding stump. It was then that the pain lanced through Blue's wilting frame. 'I don't want another dead man on my conscience. There's been enough of that to last me a lifetime.' It was an expression of regret, almost an apology.

Blue was bellyaching and moaning as if his end was nigh. 'Quit your griping, Dusty,' Bone tersely declared, tearing a strip off the kid's bandanna and tying it tightly round the injured hand. 'Mister Hogan could have easily drilled you dead centre if'n he'd chosen. Reckon you should thank him for being so generous.'

Blue was not so forgiving. All his pain-twisted maw could manage was a promise of future retribution.

29

'Some day I'll pay you off for this,' he snarled.

Hogan ignored the whining threat. 'You'll need to find him a sawbones. And while you're bandaging him up, give him a shot of whiskey. That should shut the grouchy cuss up.' He sat down on a log and poured himself a fresh cup of coffee while keeping both men covered. Rib-eye had indicated his support for Hogan's magnanimous gesture, but that didn't mean he had abandoned a desire to split the take. 'And while you're at it, Charlie, toss that hogleg over here nice and slowly. I'd hate for you to lose a finger as well. My aim might not be so good a second time.'

'Don't you trust me, boss?' the wily old brigand scoffed.

'Sure I do, Charlie. Just like I would a crafty fox.' The ex-Confederate officer's blunt manner brooked no rebuttal from his two dissenting associates. 'Now both of you shuck them boots.'

The order caught both men unawares. It was the shrewd Bone, the usual bluster knocked out of him, who voiced an obvious worry. 'You can't leave us out here with no guns! We'd be helpless as a couple of one-legged roadrunners. It ain't fair! Have a heart, Major. We've worked well together this past four years. Don't that count for something?'

'Quit your carping, Charlie,' Blue cut in with a sneer. 'This critter wants all the dough for himself with no comeback. Leaving us at the mercy of the elements so he don't have to gun us down salves his blamed conscience.'

'Don't worry yourselves, I ain't that heartless.

Though I should be, seeing as you were harbouring that notion yourself.' Hogan waved his gun, gesturing for the footwear to be discarded. 'Now hurry it up. I'll leave your gear up the trail apiece. But try coming after me and you'll both be chewing on lead sandwiches.'

With his two ex-buddies now helpless, Hogan stashed boots and weapons in the saddle-bags and gathered up the reins of their horses. 'Be seeing you boys,' he said with a brisk salute, army style. Then giving a low chuckle, he added as an afterthought, 'There again, perhaps not, eh?' Regret at having to part on such acrimonious terms, however, softened his final deliberation. 'Pity we couldn't have split up in more agreeable circumstances. I hope you'll come to accept this is the right way to use the dough.'

Blue was not so accepting. 'You can stuff that self-righteous hogwash where the sun don't shine. Keep looking over your shoulder, Hogan,' he growled out. 'Because one of these days, you'll find me there. And I won't be so damned benevolent.' He spat that final word out in the sand and turned his back.

The die was cast. But for the moment, the ball was in Hogan's court. Another curse burst from the young hot-head's mouth as he slumped down. An ugly gaze followed the alleged Judas until he disappeared from view.

'Might as well finish off this grub before we make a move,' Bone suggested with his usual shrug, accepting the cards fate had dealt him.

FOUR

SEPARATE AND DIVIDE

Around an hour later Hogan drew to a halt and dismounted. He had reached a point where the canyon he was following divided into three separate cuttings. A broad amphitheatre enclosed the rider on all sides with towering ramparts of orange sandstone. In stark contrast with the coolness of the narrow canyon from which he had just emerged, the heat out here in the open sapped all the moisture from his body.

A grey bandanna wiped away the sweat from his mottled feature as he gasped, sucking in the hot air. Lack of even the hint of breeze made the sun's influence all the more oppressive. This was not a place to linger.

Even so it provided an ideal spot in which to give his old associates a fighting chance of survival. He erected a small cairn on a ledge that was easy to spot. Rib-eye Charlie would be the one to cotton to its significance. Then he stashed the two horses and the rest of their gear behind some boulders, where a cluster of juniper trees offered cover and some forage.

As Blue had implied, it helped to salve his conscience at having abandoned them. Though not the robbery. Should he have left the money and skedaddled? The bank teller's shooting had put paid to that notion. A panic-induced trigger finger had turned the Rebel Raiders into common killers as well as outlaws facing a gallow's end. So here he was, a man alone except for his horse and a bag full of dough. He had made his choice and would see it through to the bitter end.

But that didn't prevent unsettling notions from invading his thoughts. Had he done the right thing in abandoning his old comrades? Neither had ever dropped hints about their own family circumstances. Relatives there must have been. But were they dead, or had they favoured the opposing faction during the war? A man's business was his own affair, to disclose as he saw fit, or otherwise.

Hogan was well aware that, unlike his own kinfolk, other families had been torn apart by allegiances followed during the conflict. Had Dusty and Rib-eye been right to expect some form of compensation for all the hardships suffered in the last four years? It was a dilemma that was going to haunt him for many nights to come.

For the present, however, Deke Hogan needed to make sure he disappeared to prevent his old partners from tracking him down and exacting the revenge they had promised. At least he had not added to the death toll by leaving them to die out here.

Satisfied that any guilt had been assuaged, Hogan took a piece of brushwood and secured it with his lariat to the grey mare before mounting up. No sense in giving them an easy ride. Elimination of his tracks would provide a fighting chance of thwarting any chance of their dogging his trail. He intended carrying out the same procedure for any further deviations that occurred.

Three days later the broken terrain gradually petered out, leaving Hogan facing the undulating buffalo grass country stretching north to the Colorado border. And this was where the cunning ex-guerrilla utilized the tactics that had ensured the Raiders had survived numerous successful encounters. Unlike other bands lacking imagination who had been wiped out, Major Hogan had possessed an innate ability to outwit his pursuers, so escaping to fight another day.

Rib-eye and Blue would be expecting him to head for the relative safety of No Man's Land in the Panhandle. It was the obvious course of action. So he obliged them by heading north-east towards Black Mesa. The towering monolith over forty miles distant was on the border, and the highest point in the whole of Indian Territory. Deceptively close, it was a two-day ride before he found what he was looking for.

When the clear trail faded on a patch of grey lava bed, the fugitive swung north-west, heading for Raton Pass on the Colorado border. The northern region had become a territory in 1861 at the start of the War; full statehood would not arrive for another eleven years. It was a steady climb through grandiose scenery which had seen much volcanic action in past times. Jagged peaks soared up on either side, the lava beds giving the rider confidence that his trail could not be followed by even the most assiduous tracker.

There was no sign to indicate he had crossed the border. But Hogan knew that once the ground levelled out and he began the slow descent on to the rolling plains below he was in Colorado. The territory had been a Northern enclave, so the ex-Confederate guerrilla knew he would still have to be careful not to reveal his sympathies. The Tucumcari money was intended for troops based in New Mexico, but the large sack was too conspicuous and would invite unwelcome questions. He quickly discarded it, stuffing the banknotes into his saddle-bag.

The Union forces, however, were not his only threat, and this was brought home with a vengeance as he rounded a rocky promontory. Riding straight towards him was a band of Cheyenne warriors. And they were well armed. Painted faces showed they were on a hunting expedition, notably for white scalps.

Sand Creek would be fresh in their minds. Only the previous year, the massacre of many Cheyenne, including women and children, by Union forces, had left the tribes devastated but eager for revenge. At the time, rumours of aggression by the Indians had encouraged Colonel John Chivington to attack without fear or favour. The despotic officer was described by one commentator as '*a crazy preacher who thinks he is Napoleon*'. His men responded to the 'no quarter' call with brutal and grisly efficiency, turning Sand Creek into one of the most infamous campaigns in American military history.

Deke Hogan was well aware of this iniquitous episode and the anger it had generated. If caught by these enraged redskins, he also could expect no quarter. Whoops of delight floated on the light breeze as guns and lances were raised at the sighting of this unexpected quarry. The cantering Indian ponies burst into a headlong gallop. Momentarily caught off guard, Hogan swung the grey around and headed for the nearest cover.

Pounding across the open flats, swerving between stands of mesquite and catclaw, Hogan knew he could not outrun the pursuing redskins. If anything they were gaining on him. His one chance of survival was to reach the broken terrain of the San Isobel Forest over to the west. 'Come on, old gal,' he gently coxed the tiring grey. 'I know you can make it.' Frequent looks over his shoulder displayed a different story. Yet the grey appeared to understand her master's predicament and upped the pace accordingly.

Rider and horse managed to reach the foothill

country, entering a wild landscape of dried-up arroyos and creek beds flanked by rocky banks. Swinging between the interlocking spurs he kept an eagle eye open for a chance to foil the angry pursuit. Such a situation had occurred after their defeat at Gettysburg. Fleeing the battlefield, Hogan had become separated from his men. A victory-charged squad of blue coats had chased after him. Certain death was averted when he had pulled the stunt he now hoped to emulate.

But he would have to be quick. The loyal mare was tiring fast. Around the next bend he saw his chance, and took it. Grabbing hold of the money bag and his canteen he leapt off the horse. A brisk slap on the rump, then he disappeared into a cluster of boulders. The grey galloped on, rounding the next bend just before the pursuing Indians came in sight. Hogan held his breath, watching and praying the trick would be as successful as previously.

A buzzard circled overhead, eyeing this strange man hunt. A pair of gophers were likewise intrigued. None were given any heed by the hurtling band of Cheyenne, every eagle-sharp eye being fixed on the trail ahead. They hammered past, barely ten feet from where Hogan was secreted. The ground shook, scaring the watching animals back down into their burrows.

Hogan emitted a deep sigh, realizing he had been holding his breath. But this was no time for dallying. Soon enough the redskins would discover they had been duped and retrace their steps. The fugitive had no intention of sticking around. He immediately left the trail, scrambling up the steep banking of the arroyo and setting a course towards the far side of the mountain range. It would be a long, hard climb.

But Deke Hogan was not fazed. As a veteran guerrilla fighter he was well versed in the art of living off the land. All such bands carried a survival kit comprising gear to catch fish and trap small game. The forested slopes would harbour deer and rabbits, with plenty of fast-flowing creeks hiding fish aplenty. He set a brisk pace, using his army compass to locate the next valley. Being cast afoot, he was going to need a heap of luck to back up his meagre resources.

Only half way through the month of May, the scalloped ramparts of the Sangre de Crisotos were still cloaked in a thick topping of snow. Hogan aimed for a distinctive gap in the surging wall of rock, reaching it two days later. He gave thanks that he was wearing his thick sheepskin coat, without which he would surely have frozen to death during the cold nights.

Once the sun had risen above the ribbed skyline, its heat soon warmed him up. A breakfast of spit-roasted rabbit and wild mushrooms certainly helped as well. The mountain pass known as La Vita took a full day to traverse. But at least it didn't rain, and the winds were light. The arduous trek would have been enjoyable had he not found himself in this No Man's Land of his own, a vague world of uncertainty into which fate had thrust him. What the future held was anybody's guess. All he could do now was plough on and trust that some guardian angel would direct his feet along the right trail.

Six days after losing the Cheyenne renegades, Deke Hogan finally shook off the beautiful yet wildly remote terrain of the Sangre de Cristo Mountains. He had made it down the western side in one piece by means of a handy deer track. The descent snaked through dense ranks of Ponderosa pine and Douglas fir, swinging between rocky spurs and traversing thundering creeks full of meltwater.

It had proved to be an exhausting journey, yet at the same time imbued with an atmospheric sense of euphoria. Perhaps it was the isolation, the remoteness, the notion of being at one with nature in the raw. All the same, reaching flatter ground was more than welcome. A celebration was due – his last cigar was lit and enjoyed, followed by a stick of candy hiding in the inside pocket of his coat.

The only fly in the ointment was that he now found himself facing a sprawling expanse of sand. As far as the eye could see, rolling dunes with barely a hint of greenery stretched away towards the hazy outline of the Rocky Mountains beyond. Passage over this wilderness could not be avoided. He left it until the following morning before setting off early so as to avoid the heat of the day.

Around noon for the umpteenth time, Hogan slumped down on a rock to survey the way ahead. Not a warm and friendly sight. His feet were tired and sore, though thankfully without any blisters.

Bleak, dry and inhospitable were apt descriptions of the rippling sand dunes. At least his canteen was still half full. And with a stock of dried deer meat in his pack, there was a more than even chance of making it to the mountain range on the far side. Girding up his loins, hat pulled low, he set off once again into the unknown.

Three days later and with his supplies exhausted, Hogan finally struck a well-used trail heading in a north/south direction. And judging by the ruts, it was a route used regularly by wagons and stage-coaches. Though how often they passed was a mystery. On closer inspection, the observant traveller perceived that the ruts were half full of sand, which did not augur well. Wind-blown sand could be dangerous as well as painful.

Then on cresting the next dune he came to a sudden halt, his glazed eyes widening in shocked surprise. What he saw was a bolt from the blue that he could never have anticipated.

FIVE

STAGESTRUCK!

The red and gold Concord coach stood alone, unmoving and apparently unoccupied, abandoned. Four horses were still in the traces, their heads bowed low awaiting the order to move off. So where was the driver and his passengers? Concern, anxiety that bad deeds had been perpetrated, gripped the newcomer. Revolver cocked and ready, he carefully approached the sinister enigma.

That was when he saw a body lying half hidden behind a clump of mesquite. Closer inspection drew a sharp intake of breath – a woman, and certainly dead, judging by the blood-soaked dress. She had clearly tried to escape before hot lead had chopped her down. On the far side of the coach was the bullet-riddled body of a guy who had the appearance of a sales drummer.

'What in blue blazes is this all about?' The withering epithet burst forth when he noticed the driver slumped over the brake lever, hanging there like a discarded child's doll. A macabre analogy when his boot kicked the real thing. He picked up the small mannequin whose fixed smile was totally at odds with the brutal horror its glass eyes had witnessed. The grim scenario was degenerating from bad to worse.

The coach door hung open. Hogan suspected the worst as he peered inside. What little food had congealed inside his stomach burst forth in a reflex vomit of revulsion. He turned away retching. He had seen many dead bodies in the last four years, some mutilated. But the sight of a defiled child always produced the same result. What kind of monster could resort to such depraved tactics in the name of robbery? For that was clearly what had happened here.

Coldly calculating, the pitiless brigands had just ridden off with no thought for their horrific actions, merely anticipating the high old time they would enjoy with their blood money. And they had left no witnesses to their repellent actions. The badly affected traveller needed time to recover his normal composure. He sat on a discarded piece of luggage, sucking large gulps of air into his lungs.

The Overland must have been carrying a sizeable wedge of dough to warrant this kind of mayhem. Gold letters on the door claiming association with the 'US Mail' confirmed his assumption. Rolling a querlie from the makings found in the driver's pocket, Hogan badly needed the buzz offered by the strong black tobacco. All around a thick silence pervaded the foetid air.

42

No tweeting of birds, nor the strident cawing of larger predators. Coyotes would be gathering in the hidden depths of the desert, waiting for this intruder to leave. Even now he could hear them howling to one another. Hogan scowled. 'No way are you critters gonna feast on these poor folks,' he shouted at the invisible scavengers. 'Deke Hogan will see to that.'

But without a shovel he could not bury them. Leaving the driver atop the coach he lifted the drummer into the coach followed by the woman whom he placed gently next to her daughter. That was when a piece of metal slipped from her nerveless fingers. He picked it up with a frown. 'Now what have we here?' he muttered. It was a silver and turquoise concho sporting a Comanche symbol. She must have grabbed it off one of the killers before. . . .

He stuffed it into his pocket. Once the gruesome task was complete, he muttered a few words over the bodies, set phrases taken from the officer's code of conduct. Finally, after closing the door, he rolled down the sun blinds. 'That should keep you critters away until such time as I reach the next town.'

Then he released the horses, shooing them off along the trail, but keeping hold of a chestnut for his own use. Fortunately there was a saddle strapped to the luggage rack, a Spanish-rigged Ellenberg sporting the traditional dinner-plate horn. A smart piece of kit bound for some lucky buyer. Deke Hogan commandeered it for his own use until such time as he could drop it off at the next coaching station. He was no Indian and had no intention of riding bareback.

43

With trail provisions provided by the dead driver, he moved off, leaving the macabre incident to be investigated by the authorities. Too many of his own problems were weighing down on his broad shoulders for him to become involved in someone else's misfortune.

Prophetic musings that would come back to haunt him.

Time passed in a dull haze as the lone drifter headed steadily towards the mountain barrier. Hogan gave no thought to the fate of the horses he had released. The notion that they had done this trip many times before and possessed an innate homing instinct was beyond his understanding of the cross-country transit business. As a result he had no inkling that they were all heading in the same direction, albeit along different routes. Hogan had left the main trail to avoid any unwelcome contact with other members of the human race.

Later that day as he crested the next dune he suddenly emerged from the endless sandy wasteland on to a broad flat plain. Cattle were grazing contentedly on the lush grass, and the surprised traveller could only surmise that the influence of the nearby mountain range was the cause of such an abrupt change in the nature of the landscape. A stark contrast made even more startling by the presence of a small town on the far side lying in the shelter of the mountains.

Hogan paused to look down on the pastoral scene with a guarded and somewhat perfunctory appraisal. Nobody would yet be aware of the bank hold-up south of the border. And his need for rest and recuperation following the traumatic events of the last few days was now becoming an urgent priority.

What he failed to note was the arrival of the three horses he had released after discovering the abandoned stagecoach. They had taken the main trail that entered the settlement on the far side.

A lounging Mexican sitting outside the Paradise saloon was the first to spot the horses and their strange appearance. His rheumy eyes widened beneath the broad sombrero. These were no ordinary horses, as could be clearly perceived by their long flapping reins and absent riders. The old greaser's brow furrowed in puzzlement. Something was definitely wrong here.

He levered his ageing frame out of the seat and wandered into the saloon. Peering round he spotted the man he sought: Arnold Tasker, local agent for the Overland Stage, was playing poker with his buddies when old Manuel paused beside his chair. They all ignored him.

'Hey Doc, you gonna play?' Tasker enquired of the frowning sawbones who was assiduously studying his cards. 'At this rate Harvey here will be measuring you up for a pine box.' Black-suited as befitted an undertaker, Harvey Bookbinder maintained his usual downcast regard. It was a natural guise expected from someone in his profession. And also an extra advantage, which meant he rarely lost at the weekly poker sessions held in the Paradise saloon.

45

'I already gotten your measurements, Arny,' Bookbinder expounded nonchalantly nudging his pal the sawbones. Theirs was a close association engendered through necessity as well as choice. 'And when you see what I'm holding, likely I'll be booking your place in the graveyard as well.' Chuckles all round. Only Tasker failed to see the funny side.

That was when the agent took heed of the hovering visitor snapping out, 'Something I can do for you, Manuel?'

'Stagecoach horses have arrived, senor,' the old guy declared.

'And I expect the stage is following on behind,' Tasker sniggered coughing out a derisory guffaw to throw the limelight onto the simple peasant.

'No, *señor*, no stagecoach,' was the firm reply.

Tasker frowned. 'No stagecoach you say, just horses.' It was meant to be a sarcastic putdown. More sniggers from the others. The old peon had clearly been at the tequila again.

'That is right, *señor*. Just horses.'

This time, all the men pricked up their ears. The old guy was not poking fun at them. He was serious. The card game was forgotten as the card players scrambled to their feet. Although they made sure the hands they were holding were laid face down. Along with another three men who had been listening in they hurried across to the batwing doors and peered out.

'The old timer sure wasn't joshing,' Doc Barnett declared. 'So what in tarnation has happened to the stage?' There was no reply. The conundrum had them all foxed.

'Maybe it hit a rock and broke a wheel,' suggested the fourth card player after some thought. Sowbelly Clover was a rotund pig farmer who sported the appropriate nickname with pride. He was a simple jasper easy to read in a card game. But there was no doubting the quality of the porkers he raised and the bacon sold in the local butcher's shop.

Tumbleweed rushed by, driven on by the moaning wind that had sprung up. Sand was being whipped up into spiralling eddies, blurring the visibility. Another storm was brewing. Late spring was the time the mountains flexed their muscles after the long winter.

'That don't tell us why the driver released the horses,' said Tasker, only managing to intensify the disturbing incident. 'And why only three, our smaller coaches are always drawn by four horses?' The mystery had deepened.

'My new saddle should be on that stage,' grumbled the undertaker, more concerned about the property for which he had already paid. 'A fine Ellenberg I ordered specially from Denver. I hope it ain't been stolen.' He would soon find out.

Arnold Tasker's eyes bulged wide with anxiety. 'You don't think the stage has been robbed, do you?' he spluttered out, the blood draining from his face. 'The strong box was carrying a heap of dough to pay off the miners up in Contention.'

Nobody had any answers to that conundrum, nor

did they wish to voice an opinion. The three loose animals held their attention, waiting patiently outside the stagecoach office.

Up on the rim overlooking the town, Deke Hogan continued his vigil, ignorant of the events being played out below. He was no longer in the first flush of youth, far from it. The war was over. All he wanted to do now was return to his home state of Missouri, deposit the bank haul in the most appropriate hands to aid the South's reconstruction, then settle down to a quiet life. And that objective would only be achieved by heading due east from here across the prairie grassland of Kansas to Topeka, from where he could catch a train. All he need do was keep a sharp eye open for bands of roaming Comanches.

A barb of uncertainty lanced through his taut frame. Two years had passed since he had last been home. Had his ageing parents managed to survive the brutal conflict? He brushed aside the chilling reality that many southern folk had suffered. Travelling down that road would only lead to despair. Optimism had always been his byword, and so it would remain until such time as the truth was unearthed.

Before entering the unknown settlement, he decided to conceal the bag of money beneath a rock adjacent to a prominent buttress having the appearance of a giant bodkin. No sense taking chances of having it stolen while he slept. He would recover it on leaving town.

Nudging the chestnut down a slope, he cantered across the rangeland but stopped on the edge of the town, nervous about venturing into the first hint of civilization since the flight from Tucumcari. Painted bright red, a sign informed him he had reached Glory Be – population 854, elevation 5,267 feet.

The newcomer's leathery face cracked in a brief smile on spotting a pool of water ensconced within a girdle of rocks. He could readily understand the origin of such a name clearly designated by a grateful traveller who had stumbled upon the life-saving elixir. A well complete with lever-action pump stood to one side. Hogan doused his head of the thick coating of dust stuck to his skin, following up with a much needed drink. It felt good.

Unlike many frontier townships, this one appeared to be of Spanish origin, judging by the proliferation of adobe structures. Maybe that was for protection against the stiff northerly that had suddenly blown up. One minute calm and quiet reigned supreme, the next a roaring howler slammed into his back. Yet another consequence tossed down from the heights behind the town.

Hogan pulled his hat down and pushed on, walking the horse down the main street as racing clumps of tumbleweed passed him by. A saloon boasting the appropriate handle of Windy Wilf's caught his attention. It was situated a couple of blocks down from the Paradise on the far side. A drink or three

together with some decent grub was sorely needed.
He guided the horse over to the hitching rail.

But his presence had not passed unnoticed.

SIX

STRANGER THAN FICTION

'Who's that over yonder?' Sowbelly was the first to spot the hazy form of a rider coming down the street, albeit from a different direction to the stage horses. Strangers always attracted attention in remote frontier townships. And Glory Be was well off the regular trails. Normally they were eagerly accosted for news of the outside world. But today, these men had other, more pressing issues on their minds.

The baffled spectators remained behind the saloon door, not wishing to venture out into the burgeoning gale, and more likely not wishing to challenge the shadowy stranger. So the question was meaningless and ignored. Observed through the swirling belts of sand, any chance of putting a name to a blurred face was as likely as Sowbelly walking

51

away from a poker game boasting a smile.

It was Tasker who delivered a decidedly cogent remark that elicited nervous gasps from his buddies. 'Never seen him before,' he declared. 'But I sure recognize that chestnut horse he's riding. It's the fourth one from the team.'

'Could be this guy is the thief,' Harvey Bookbinder contended. 'That's a new Ellenberg he's a-sitting on.' Nobody moved. None of the card players were over-eager to confront what could be a ruthless brigand. They all looked sheepishly at one another. 'Who's gonna go out there and confront him?' enquired the nervous coaching agent, pertinently aware that this was really his responsibility. But tackling a possible gunman was another thing entirely, and not included in his job description.

All eyes then followed Tasker's lead as he turned towards a lone drinker leaning on the far end of the bar. Marshal Ike Stanford's thoughts were elsewhere. He was being pressured by the town council to do something about the robberies that were plaguing Saguache County. Over the last few months three coaches had been held up, and the passengers robbed of their money and valuables. On two occasions gold bullion being transferred from mines based at Contention and Cotopaxi had substantially added to the robbers' illicit haul.

Stanford had followed up leads, but none had so far resulted in any arrests, and folks were getting edgy. Business would suffer if this continued, and Stanford would be held accountable. If those blamed councillors had agreed to him taking on a deputy, he would have more chance of tracking the jaspers. But Elias Jacoby, the town's bank manager and leader of the council, had claimed that a small town like Glory Be couldn't afford the added expense. So he was stymied. The lawman slung down another shot of whiskey, his brow furrowing in exasperation.

'Ain't you heard a thing we been saying, Ike?' Tasker snapped walking over to confront the lounging lawman. 'The stage is missing and there's some guy out there riding one of the team.'

'And we want to know what you're gonna do about it,' butted in Sowbelly, hitching up his sagging pants. 'We figure he might have robbed the stage and stranded the passengers out there in the desert.'

Only then did the lawman deign to look round. His watery eyes rolled. It was clear he had supped more than just one drink. The bottle resting by his elbow was half empty. He levered himself off the bar, attempting to shake the mush from his head. 'Only one guy, you say?' he enquired. 'Don't see how one man could have robbed a stagecoach on his ownsome.' It was a reasonable assumption. He walked over to the door, the words slurring together as he peered out into the gloom. Hogan had just dismounted. 'Guess I'd better wander across and see what's going on.'

The marshal stopped midway across the street, eyeing the newcomer and drew his revolver. Hogan was undoing the straps on his saddlebag, oblivious to the nearby presence. He was looking forward to a good meal and a decent night's sleep in a bed. Just as he made to step up on to the boardwalk, the racking back of the gun hammer to full cock alerted all his senses to the danger.

His immediate conclusion was that somehow those two jiggers had managed to track him down. Why else would somebody be pulling a gun on him in this remote berg? And Dusty Blue had threatened to shoot him down on the spot.

There was only one response possible under those circumstances. Without thinking he threw himself to one side and spun round. At the same time his own revolver was palmed. Both guns spat flame at one and the same moment. But the drink had slowed Stanford, and the bullet from his gun whistled by, smashing Windy Wilf's front window.

Hogan's reply was well placed. The lawman clutched at his shoulder and went down. The winner of the showdown hurried across, his gun at the ready in case of any subterfuge. On more than one occasion in the past, an adversary had played possum, trying to gain the advantage.

He rolled the comatose body over on to its back, gun cocked and ready to deliver the solution to any chicanery. But Stanford was not play acting and was well out of the fight. Thankfully he was still alive, although quite badly injured. What caught Hogan's attention more than anything, however, was the tin star pinned to his chest. He gulped, his thumping heart lurching. A damned lawman! Could his luck get any worse? The cat was now well and truly out of the bag.

The gunfire had attracted the attention of more citizens, not least those drinking in Windy Wilf's. 'What in blue blazes is all the shooting about?' shouted the saloon owner, Wilf Jenner. 'Some critter is gonna have to pay for that window!'

Hogan immediately pumped a couple of slugs above the heads of the crowd, adding to the damage and driving the gathering crowd back into the saloon. But the shooting down of their marshal, not to mention the appearance of more men, had strengthened the backbones of Arnold Tasker and his cronies.

'Get the varmint!' shouted Bookbinder, aiming a couple of shots at the hazy figure across the street. But they were well wide of the mark. These men were not hard-boiled gunfighters. Hogan knew he had to get off the main street. He dashed off in the opposite direction. 'Let's get after him, boys, before he escapes,' the undertaker added. He paused beside the stolen horse. 'I was right about this being an Ellenberg saddle. It must be mine, and that critter stole it.'

They had now been joined by those from the other saloon. 'We'll split up,' Jenner declared, taking control of the situation. 'You fellas from the Paradise go that way by the church, and we'll go round by the clinic. That way we should trap him in a pincer movement.' The saloon owner had been a captain with the 4th Colorado Volunteers during the war.

Tasker was more than happy to pass the responsibility of decision making to someone else. 'OK boys, let's go.' Hogan had now disappeared down an alley. 'Anybody see which way he went?' The swirling cloud of dry sand was a hindrance to a clear sighting of their quarry.

'He must have turned off along Chama Lane, next to the dressmaker's,' Sowbelly suggested. With the pig farmer in the lead, they headed off that way. Strength in numbers stiffened their resolve to catch the perpetrator of the heinous shooting. Hogan stopped at the end of the narrow passageway, unsure which way to go. 'There he is!' The hazy outline was spotted by Tasker, who fired off a couple of shots. 'Get after him, boys. The skunk can't get far.'

Hogan ducked down as the bullets whistled by overhead. He could hear the other group of pursuers coming down a parallel alley two blocks east of where he was hiding behind a water barrel. At this rate he would soon be blocked in. The noisy clamour from his pursuers told of a grim reception should he be caught, with a rope's end the most likely result.

Staying put was not an option. He pumped a couple of shots from his own revolver along Chama Lane to delay Sowbelly and his buddies. The delaying tactic provided a brief respite, giving him valuable seconds to slip down a track slanting off at an angle between more buildings. One man against upwards of a dozen or more irate citizens eager for his blood is apt to focus that man's thoughts. Panic now, and Hogan knew that he would be lost.

Judging by the angry shouts in front, a third cluster of hunters appeared to have joined in the chase. And all of them were closing in fast. Under such dire circumstances, the dust storm was his only friend. But for how long? It could only be a matter of time before he was hunted down. Trapped with nowhere to go, his whole body tensed as he caught a sliver of movement at the far end of the passage.

Thankfully it was only another cluster of tumble-weeds banging against each other like panic-stricken sheep cornered by a timber wolf. Deke Hogan felt much the same as his addled brain desperately tried to figure a way out.

Just then a shadow-filled alcove loomed out of the murk. He ducked into the recess, breathing hard, but grateful to have the reassuring embrace of obscurity. His hand rested on the door handle, and the door, much to his surprise, swung inwards. Hogan took advantage of this Heaven-sent piece of good fortune and stepped inside, quickly closing the door behind him. His luck was still in. The room was empty.

And he was only just in time. Muted voices met outside the recess, arguing forcefully about how to locate their illusive prey. Hogan held his breath, praying they would not suspect he was only feet from where they stood. Moments later the gabbling throng moved off to continue the search elsewhere. A whoosh of air billowed from between tight lips; a silent plea of thanks despatched to the Man upstairs for his salvation from mob vengeance.

But had his relief come too soon? A light came on in the adjoining room, accompanied by raised voices.

57

Had he jumped from the frying pan into the fire? Unlike the hysterical uproar redolent of the vengeance seekers, these voices were controlled, if of a somewhat querulous nature. Hogan turned back to exit the building, hoping to find another way out of the mess into which he had unwittingly stumbled. But his intentions were brought to a sudden halt, when he heard the faint but unmistakable mention of a stagecoach.

His ears pricked up. Could they be discussing the absent Overland he himself had come across only the day before? Hogan stepped closer to the glass-partitioned door. Painted in gothic script was the heading '*Glory Be Land Agency and Bank:* manager Elias Jacoby'. The thick walls and door had clearly deadened the hullabaloo outside. But that also meant he could not hear the animated discussion being conducted inside the office.

'What in thunder possessed you to kill those people?' an aggressively deep voice demanded. Elias Jacoby jumped to his feet. Pudgy hands gripped the edges of his desk. 'All you were meant to do was scare them a little, grab the dough then hightail it out of there.'

'We didn't have any choice when that darned driver pulled my mask down and recognized me, the woman as well.' The belligerent speaker was a hard-nosed gunman, ostensibly hired as a bank guard. In reality he was an outlaw wanted across three states for robbery and murder. Latigo Rennick appeared unabashed by the rebuke. 'They all knew who I worked for. And I'm sure you wouldn't have wanted that to become public knowledge, would you?'

The gunman's claim was backed by his sidekick. 'It's like Latigo says, boss,' Nevada Bass Tiptree affirmed. 'We weren't given any choice.' Both killers shrugged off the banker's concern. The outcome of the unfortunate incident was obvious. 'So they all had to go.'

Jacoby was desperately seeking some way out of the dire predicament his lackeys' reckless action had caused. His brow creased in thought, frantic to find a plausible explanation for the official investigation that would follow such a heinous crime. 'If'n the Pinkertons are brought in they could uncover much more than any of us would want,' he asserted nervously.

'We could always say it was a Comanche raiding party. Those critters are always breaking out of the reservation,' the fourth man in the room anxiously suggested. Howard Kemper, a well dressed land speculator, was the oldest of the trio and the most nervous. Greying hair and a white beard gave him a benign look that people found trusting. He had quickly learned to use this innate attribute for his own subversive gain. The crooked businessman nervously dabbed at his sweating face.

Latigo hawked out a scornful guffaw. His lower lip curled down at one side, a look he had cultivated to intimidate those who questioned his methods. 'Indians always scalp their victims. You fellas can always go back there and finish the job. If'n you have the stomach, that is.' Hard flinty eyes, cold as ice, fastened on to the corpulent banker and his associate as he casually lit up a cigar. 'Anyway, what you guys worrying about? We got the dough, didn't we?'

'That does it!' Kemper bleated waving his hands about. 'I didn't come in with you, Elias, to become involved with murder. Those other robberies were OK. Nobody was hurt. But a woman and child . . .' Kemper's breathing was growing more laboured as panic set in. 'That's too damned much to accept. I'm getting out. You can keep my share of the money. I don't want to be associated with it.'

Jacoby threw a meaningful look towards his two bodyguards. 'Now hold on there, Howard,' the banker declared, trying to keep his irritation under control. Any panic-induced action from this scared rabbit could land them all in trouble. 'Don't be forgetting that we're all in this together. If'n we stick to the same story, there's no reason for anybody to suspect who was behind this catastrophe.'

But Kemper was not to be swayed. He'd got a bad case of the jitters. His nerves were shattered and it showed in his twitchy features. 'The county sheriff will be down here lickety split when he learns what's happened. It'll be headline news across the whole territory. Robberies are one thing. Indiscriminate murder is a whole different ball game. They won't leave a stone unturned until they find the culprits.' He turned to leave. 'I'm getting out of here, right now.'

Jacoby knew his partner had become a dangerous

liability. A brisk look of accord passed between Jacoby and the gunmen. Latigo knew exactly what had to be done. His hand rested on the gun butt.

At that very same moment Hogan realized he needed to take cover. What little he had heard was sufficient for him to appreciate that one of the men was about to leave. He backed away from the door as Howard Kemper stamped across the room.

That was when Lady Luck decided she had been too generous to the fugitive.

SEVEN

REFUGE IN A STORM

Hogan accidently tripped over a spittoon. The crooks inside the adjoining office could not fail to hear the echoing clang. 'There's somebody out there,' Jacoby hollered, his previous composure abandoned. Kemper was nearest the door, which he flung open. 'Who's there?' he croaked out.

Hogan just managed to hide behind a desk on the far side of the room when the businessman appeared in the doorway, a dark silhouette starkly outlined against the yellow light of the office. Those were Howard Kemper's last words as a shot rang out. Arms raised, he pitched forwards, staggered a couple of paces, then tumbled in a heap on the floor.

Jacoby immediately filled the gap left by the dead man. Immediately behind him, a smoking gun in his right hand, stood Latigo. Anticipating he would be trapped like a rat up a drainpipe if he remained where he was, Hogan knew he had to get out of there. The crooks had momentarily been stunned by the shock of having been eavesdropped. But they would soon recover. It was lucky for him that the back room was in darkness.

He pitched a couple of shots at the open door, smashing the glass panel and driving the two villains back inside. At the same time he lunged for the back door emerging on to the alleyway. A couple of bullets from Latigo followed him. But they went wide as Hogan disappeared from view, no more than a shadowy wraith.

Thankfully, nobody was in sight. That said, the gunfire would undoubtedly draw the attention of the searching multitude, so he needed to find a bolt hole rapidly. A block further along and he heard the sound of raised voices. The militant crowd were heading his way. He dropped behind a stack of boxes, the churning sand helping to mask his presence as the mob rushed by.

Jacoby and the bodyguard were standing in the open doorway when the crowd arrived, led by Arnold Tasker. They were breathing hard, and tempers were frayed on account of the fruitless pursuit. 'We heard the gunfire and came a-running,' Tasker gasped out. 'What happened?'

'A man just broke into the bank and tried to rob us at gunpoint,' Jacoby declared firmly. 'When I refused to open the safe, my guard tried to disarm him. But the skunk shot and killed Howard Kemper. The poor guy was unarmed and didn't stand a chance.' The explanation was readily accepted. Nobody had any reason to think otherwise.

'This must be the same fella that held up the stage. The driver must have shot his horse before being killed. Then he released the other horses to give him a chance to get away,' Tasker added. 'He has to be hiding around here.'

'And he also shot the marshal,' Sowbelly called out. 'The poor jasper is lucky to be alive.'

A well respected citizen in Glory Be, the banker immediately took charge of the shambolic chase. 'The best thing to do is organize a proper search. I suggest we all meet up at Wilf's place in ten minutes. Groups of men can then be allocated to different parts of the town. That way we can cover every nook and cranny. Don't worry boys, we'll soon flush him out.'

It was a good ploy from the devious villain, and received eager nods of agreement. 'We're all with you on that, Elias,' the saloon owner declared vigorously. 'This guy has already gunned down two men in town. He'll be desperate enough to kill others now. The sooner we have him locked up the better.'

'That's right,' Sowbelly piped up. 'Ain't none of us safe with a deadly killer like that on the loose.'

Jacoby smiled to himself. His final request was to the undertaker. 'I'd much appreciate it, Harvey, if'n you could arrange for poor Howard's body to be moved to the mortuary. God rest his soul.' He removed his hat in respect, assuming a suitably mournful demeanour. Everyone present immediately followed suit. 'Howard Kemper was more than just a business partner, he was a good friend who will be sorely missed.'

Nods of agreement all round. Jacoby knew he had these scared rabbits in the palm of his hand. Back inside the bank, he rubbed his hands with cynical satisfaction. 'This couldn't have come at a better time, boys. All the robberies will now be attributed to this fella, putting us in the clear.'

'And more dough to share out, with Kemper out of the picture,' Tiptree leered.

'Just so long as we catch the guy and shut him up for keeps,' Latigo stated, knowing his neck was on the line should the truth emerge. 'We don't know how much he heard.'

'Maybe he didn't hear anything,' Jacoby replied impatiently. 'And at least he can't identify us.'

Latigo dismissed his paymaster with a brusque huff of derision. The scornful rebuttal brought a tight-lipped growl from the banker. He was used to being treated with deference, high regard, especially from an employee. But he held his temper in check. He needed the gun-toting ability of these hardcases – and more so now than ever, following this lethal disruption to their well-laid scheme. Everything had being going so well until this stranger had blundered into the mêlée, threatening to wreck the whole deal. He had to be found and eliminated.

Rennick was equally aware of the truth that Jacoby

needed his protection. Ignoring the banker's simmering rancour, he posed the logical dilemma. 'What you're forgetting is that we can't identify him neither. Only person to see him up close was the marshal.'

'And in this sand storm, it's unlikely he could give a good description,' added Tiptree. 'If'n he ain't caught soon, the critter could ride down the street and nobody would know him from Adam. Just another drifter heading for the gold fields.'

Jacoby strove to reassert his authority. A coldly potent look pinned the two bank guards to the spot. 'We can't take the chance that he didn't hear anything. It's up to you fellas to ensure this doesn't come to trial. Last thing we need is him sticking his nose where it don't belong. And remember that anybody you don't recognize is a suspect.'

Latigo drew his revolver, a nickel-plated Manhattan, and spun the chamber. 'Don't you worry none, boss. Me and Nevada will soon hunt him down.' He pointed the revolver at a portrait of the banker himself gracing the wall behind his desk. 'Then it'll be bang, bang, you're dead.' Mirthless guffaws assailed the ashen-faced banker. 'And once he's bit the dust we can get back to how things should be around here. And nobody will be any the wiser.'

With Kemper out of the frame, Latigo was rapidly arriving at the conclusion that he should be made a fifty-fifty partner in their nefarious schemes. When he had gotten rid of this meddling stranger, he would make sure that Jacoby was not given any choice in the matter.

A short time later, Elias Jacoby's managerial skills had taken over. Almost every able-bodied man in town had answered his summons, not least because of the circulating rumour that a reward was on offer for the alleged killer's capture. The diligent hunters were arranged into separate teams. Each group was to search a different section of the town.

'Don't worry, men. We'll run this skunk down in no time,' he assured the gathering. 'Make sure to search every yard so we cover the whole town.' His last order before the men departed was designed to ensure his two bodyguards locked the miscreant up in the jail. 'My bank guard Mister Rennick will take charge of the search.' Nobody objected, such was Jacoby's influence. 'He must be informed the moment this man is captured. Is that clear? We need to make this an official arrest. There will be no vigilante law in Glory Be.'

The drinkers were more than happy to comply. And much to everyone's delight the report hinting of monetary incentive proved to be no idle piece of gossip. 'And after he's been locked up, come back here and we'll have a proper celebration. And the team that makes the arrest will earn themselves a good bonus.' Cheers all round. Everybody loved a party when somebody else was footing the bill. And the bonus was the icing on the cake.

The object of their exhilaration was tired and crestfallen, having taken refuge inside an enclosed yard filled with bags of oatmeal. Hogan slumped down on a pile of empty sacking as he struggled to accept the dire predicament into which he had unwittingly blundered. Outside the storm rumbled on, snapping and bawling like an angry hound dog tethered against its will.

Inside the temporary shelter offered by the yard, relative calm ensued. At least for the moment Hogan felt he had been given some respite, the chance to figure out how best to extricate himself from the chaos. His eyes flickered as fatigue enveloped his weary frame. Even under such horrendous circumstances, the human body can only keep going for so long before it shuts down. That moment had arrived.

In seconds he was asleep. Unfortunately, the escape from reality can only have been brief. He was awoken by angry shouts on the far side of the fence enclosing the small yard. Hogan tensed, holding his breath. Were the hunters about to snatch their prey? If so he would go down fighting. Nobody was going to string him up for someone else's crime. He palmed the Remington, gripping the bone handle so hard his knuckles blanched.

'Don't look like he's around here,' one voice declared urgently. 'You three go down there, and we'll head off this way. He has to be around here somewhere, and we want to be the ones grabbing that bonus.' For some unaccountable reason, this bunch of searchers had ignored the yard. But others could be along at any second. And next time he might not be so lucky. A quick peep outside revealed an empty back lot.

Raised voices urging each other onwards could still be heard, but their location was impossible to pin down in the frenetic hollering of the gale. All sound became disembodied, vague and illusive reverberations ricocheting between the haphazard collection of buildings.

Hogan knew that he had to find a more secure place to hide out until such time as he could leave this damned place behind. Gingerly he emerged from the yard's comforting refuge, scuttling along behind a low wall. More echoing voices filtered through the thick miasma. He leapt over the wall, crouching down, wondering which way to go. Panic was rapidly threatening to engulf his customary resilience.

His boot heel caught against an iron ring, a hollow clunk informing his churning brain that he was standing on the entrance to a cellar or underground room. Perhaps this was the sanctuary he was seeking?

Hope surged in his breast as he slowly raised the hatch, praying that no squealing hinges betrayed his presence. All remained quiet as he peered down into the gloom. Little could be discerned. But at least nobody was down there. Quickly the fugitive lowered himself to the ground below, reaching up to close the hatch. Moments later the thudding of feet drew near to the hideout. They did not pause, passing onwards to continue the search elsewhere.

A small aperture high on the wall allowed some light to penetrate the chamber, revealing a clean cellar used for storing dried and bottled produce for the occupants of the premises above ground. Over on the far side was a stack of bridles, stirrups, saddle skirts and a host of other paraphernalia, testifying to this being a saddle shop.

But it was a slab of smoked pork hanging up that caught his attention. Extracting a knife, he sliced off a few lean pieces and slapped them between some freshly baked bread set on a table. It tasted delicious, and was polished off in the blink of an eye. For dessert he took some peaches from one of the jars. He felt much better following this impromptu repast.

A door led through to an adjacent room. On entering he was faced with a flight of stone steps leading up to the main part of the building. But his sudden presence had been noted by a couple of tiny puppies that had been sleeping in a basket. They immediately began yapping. This was the last thing Hogan needed. He desperately tried shushing the noisy pair, to no avail.

Then lo and behold, the door at the top of the stairs swung open. Hogan just managed to conceal himself behind the door in the other room. Through the gap he observed a woman descending the stairs. Even under such taxing conditions he could not fail to admire the elegant sway of the hips, the long glossy tresses and smoothly aquiline features of the building's resident.

Under any other circumstances he would have welcomed her sudden appearance into his life. As it was, he was an intruder into her home, a suspected gun-slinging robber. The identifying object of his profession was held ready – though the matter of what he would do with it should she suspect his presence was best left to speculation.

The woman's attention was naturally drawn to her dogs. 'What's all this racket for?' she gently chided the two culprits. Then she assumed the reason, and nodded an understanding. 'So that supper I gave you wasn't enough. You two will get fat with all this pampering being handed out.' She lifted up the basket. 'I'll take you both upstairs where I can keep an eye on you.' Fussing over the small bundles of fur, she turned about and headed back up the stairs.

EIGHT

CAUGHT OUT

Once again the cellar was quiet. Hogan blew out a sigh of relief. He drank some of the peach juice, then sat down on a cot laid out in an alcove, surmising that it must be used by the proprietor for overnight stays in the store. He did not stop to think that this would be such a night. Overwhelmed by the ordeal of recent days, all he wanted to do was lie down on the bed and sleep for a month.

His eyes closed almost before his head touched the pillow. Above Hogan's head, Lucy Courtright had set the basket down and was tending to another dependent who was sprawled out on a bed in the living room behind the store. Her father Ezra had suffered a broken leg when he fell off a wild mustang he had been trying to tame on the family smallholding out in Lodge Pole Canyon.

The leg had broken in three places and was causing him a lot of pain. 'You should never have

mounted that angry critter at your age,' she casti-
gated the mule-headed old man while changing the
dressings. An attempt to conceal the concern evident
on her ashen face failed miserably. Doc Barnett had
told her in confidence that even at best Ezra would
be left with a bad limp.

Already they were being harried by the bank for
repayment of a loan to buy the horse ranch. The
horses they had sold to the army had only brought in
sufficient money to cover the interest on the loan.
With her father unable to manage the ranch, they
had been thrown back on surviving off the takings
from the saddle business. And with another, similar
concern having recently opened at the far end of
town, takings were only enough to cover everyday
expenses.

A tear dribbled down the girl's cheek. She quickly
brushed it off, not wishing her father to witness the
anguish bubbling up inside her. 'We'll soon have you
up and in the saddle again, Pa,' she assured the
injured man, who was chafing at the bit to do just
that. 'But you need to rest up if'n that leg is going to
heal.'

'It was just bad luck, that mean cuss tossing me off
like that,' Ezra asserted, anxious to shift the blame
off his own shoulders. The old rancher did not want
to admit he was past his best, over the hill. 'He
caught me off guard. It sure won't happen again.'
That was a truth Lucy knew well enough, but for
reasons that were different from those assumed by
her father.

'You get some sleep, Pa,' she said settling him down. 'The doc will be here in the morning to check you out. Let's just wait and see what he has to say.'

Ezra gave a disparaging grunt as he tried to lift himself up on one elbow. 'That butcher will have me on crutches. Well, it ain't gonna happen, gal. I'll show that old coot I ain't finished yet, not by a long chalk.' The vehement tirade brought on a wince of pain from the inflamed leg.

Lucy calmed him down before retiring to the parlour, where she could let the flood gates of her anxiety open. How were they going to manage with her father unable to work? She hadn't had the heart to tell him she had been forced to release the rest of the horses back into the wild. All that remained were the small fields of ripening crops.

But the girl was resilient, and quickly pulled herself together. Living on the frontier, with none of the comforts advertised in those eastern society magazines that occasionally found their way west, made it essential for womenfolk to shoulder a heavy burden of responsibility. Many whom she met on a daily basis bore the physical strain of eking out a precarious life on the frontier.

Lucy was an attractive woman who had no intention of succumbing to a life of back-breaking toil, growing old before her time. Numerous attempts had been made to corral her without success. When the right man came along she would know. Until then, she would do her best under the difficult state of affairs that were looming.

But it was tough work. All her reserves of spirit and determination had to be constantly brought to bear. Once again she opened the letter from Elias Jacoby, reminding her that the sum outstanding on the loan was overdue. The smarmy banker had dished out hints on more than one occasion as to how she could extricate herself from the dilemma. The thought of those sinuous hands pawing at her flesh made the girl shiver with revulsion. Death would be a more acceptable option.

Unbeknown to Lucy Courtright, due to the ferocity of the storm, she was totally oblivious to the grim pursuit going on around her. Yet no matter how diligent the hunters ferreted and delved, no sign of the fugitive could be found. It was with downcast faces that each of the search teams finally returned to Windy Wilf's where Elias Jacoby was anxiously awaiting news that he hoped would lay his apprehension to rest. Namely the report that the alleged killer had been shot while resisting arrest.

There was to be no such declaration. Their woebegone expressions spoke volumes. 'The boys tried their best,' Arnold Tasker apologized. 'But in this darned storm we can hardly see a thing. He could be anywhere.' The others were equally disheartened, more due to the lack of a reward and the promised celebration.

Jacoby gritted his teeth, attempting to remain calm and in control. 'We'll start up again first thing in the morning. Hopefully by then the storm will have blown itself out. The critter must still be holed up in town somewhere. Nobody could have escaped in this squall.' He turned away, allowing his face to assume a withering look of anger threaded with a measure of fear. His beady eyes narrowed to thin slits: this fella had to be caught and eliminated.

A curt nod of the head saw the bartender pushing a full bottle of scotch his way as the men slunk off. The bite of the hard liquor was badly needed. 'Don't forget, first thing in the morning, boys,' he threw after them over his shoulder. 'That bonus still stands.'

Hogan awoke next morning to the sound of feet shuffling about over his head. For a moment his brain could not figure out what he was doing there. Then it all came charging back like a rampant stampede of cattle. The abandoned stagecoach, the shooting of a lawman, followed by his stumbling on some inexplicable skulduggery in the bank. And lastly the pursuit that had found him skulking down in this cellar like some frightened prairie dog.

To have hit the Tucumcari bank ostensibly as a military target only to discover he had become nought but a common criminal was bad enough. But to have the citizens of this place wanting to string him up when he was totally innocent just rubbed salt into the wound. He staggered over to a water pump and doused his head to help clear the feeling of injustice. The need to escape from this town as quickly as possible became an urgent priority.

But first he needed some food. Another beef sandwich and the rest of those delicious peaches hit the spot. With the inner man satisfied, he crept up the stairs and emerged into a corridor. Nobody was about. The person he had heard appeared to have gone out. Slowly he moved towards the door. The need to secure a horse could be faced once he was outside.

That was when he almost walked into the woman he had seen the night before. And she was even lovelier to behold in the light of day. Hers was a natural beauty, a gift that few other women on the frontier could match. There was none of the paint that saloon gals daubed across their faces: meant to ensnare paying clients, their artificial means to entice only served to make this woman even more alluring in the eyes of Deke Hogan.

Neither of them spoke, both startled by the sudden encounter. The woman was the first to recover her composure. 'What are you doing, sneaking around in my house?' she demanded, though more out of curiosity than with any hint of fear. She sniffed imperiously, not waiting for an answer. Floating locks of hair stirred like a field of ripe corn. 'And if'n you intend using that gun, just get on with it. I can't stop you.' A challenge had been laid down.

Hogan was taken aback by this unusually feisty retaliation. He looked at the pointed weapon and quickly replaced it in his holster. 'S-sorry about that, m-ma'am,' he stuttered, red-faced. 'Forgetting my manners. I was just leaving.'

She barred his way. 'Not before you answer my question.'

'I was caught out in the storm last night and took shelter in the cellar,' he replied regaining some measure of dignity. 'I couldn't get out that way because the trap door was covered in sand. And I'm obliged to you for the peaches.'

Another sniff from the woman, although this time it was accompanied by the hint of a smile. 'I trust you enjoyed them?'

'Best I ever tasted. And the beef sandwich went down a treat as well.'

This added extra produced a raised eyebrow. The addition of a curled lip was meant to be reproachful, but sent shivers through the intruder's taut frame. 'You certainly appear to have made yourself at home,' she stated rather loftily imbuing the comment with a hint of irony. 'Perhaps you would like me to cook you some breakfast before you leave?'

The curt statement was meant as a sarcastic jibe, but was received with nonchalant ease by the handsome stranger, who came back with a crafty smirk of his own: 'That's mighty generous of you, ma'am. Naturally I'm willing to pay you the going rate for my board and accommodation.'

Before the girl could respond, there was a loud knock on the door.

NINE

GUARDIAN ANGEL

Both of them tensed. Hogan drew his pistol, ushering the girl towards a nearby window. 'See who it is, then send them away,' he hissed, once again assuming the unwelcome role of the skulking fugitive. 'And remember I've got this. And I ain't afraid to use it.'

Lucy shivered at the sight of the bleak face clutching the deadly Remington before gingerly pulling back a curtain. 'It's Doc Barnett. He's here to see my father, who's been badly injured in a riding accident. I'll have to let him in or he'll become suspicious.' Once again her tone became accusatory. 'I take it you have good reason for not wanting to be seen?'

'Just answer the door if'n you must, lady,' he rasped, ignoring the question as he ducked behind a closet door. 'Just try and get rid of him. But remember I'll be listenin' to every word. One false move and. . . .' He left the threat hanging in the air, not wishing to carry it through. The last thing he wanted was more killing to add to those that these people had thrown his way.

Lucy opened the door, then just stood there, unsure how to proceed. 'Well aren't you going to let me in, Lucy?' the doctor asked quizzically, eyeing the comely daughter of his patient. 'You did ask me to call round this morning, if'n you recall.'

Remembering the gun aimed at her back, she had no option but to usher the sawbones inside. 'Pa's upstairs,' she said, following behind but casting wary glances towards the closet. Hogan meantime was on tenterhooks. Unable to do anything but wait, he had no idea what was being discussed in the closed room upstairs. It could all be about the injured man. On the other hand she might well be informing the visitor of his presence in the house.

After pealing back the old dressing, the doctor muttered to himself, struggling to keep the anxiety from his face. A beard specially cultivated for such diagnoses helped to conceal his concern. 'I'll give you some tablets for the pain. Then I'll redress the break,' he said, before wagging a reproachful finger at the patient as he warily examined the ugly wound. 'You're getting too old for bronc busting, Ezra. It's a young man's game. I don't know what you were thinking, buying that ranch at your age. Ain't farming enough for you? '

'Not you as well, Doc,' the old man grumbled. 'I get enough carping from Lucy. I'll be OK once you've done your job and set this thing. Nothing is gonna keep me down.'

The medic gave that remark a look of disbelief, shaking his head while tying off the fresh dressing. 'I ain't so sure about that. We'll get you over to the surgery later today so's I can fit a plaster cast. You'll need plenty of rest for this injury to heal. No horse riding. Understand?'

After leaving the room he pulled Lucy aside and sketched out his depressing prognosis in a hoarse whisper. 'I'm afraid it's a lot worse than when I last called.' He paused, swallowing before delivering the bad news. 'My figuring is that infection has set in. It's gonna need some special ointment, and that don't come cheap.' He fixed a quizzical eye on the girl, knowing that their finances were stretched to the limit.

'Don't worry about payment, doc,' she assured him. 'I'll find it somehow.'

'He should be all right if'n I can stem the infection before it spreads,' Barnett continued. 'But it may well come down to an amputation.'

Lucy was mortified. A hand rose to cover her mouth. The doctor laid a comforting hand on her shoulder. 'I'll do what I can. Hopefully we'll have caught it in time.' Deep down the medic feared the worst, but his eyes conveyed a message of optimism and encouragement.

Eventually they both came down the stairs. Hogan followed their every move. Doc Barnett appeared to be totally unaware of his threatening presence. But there again, it could all be a ploy so that he could leave the house and raise the alarm. Ears keenly attuned to every nuance in the medic's discourse, Hogan listened in.

Barnett was about to leave, much to the fugitive's relief, when he paused. 'Do you have any guns in the house?' Mention of firearms turned the girl's face white. 'I don't want to scare you, but there's a desperado loose in town. He shot down the sheriff before trying to rob the bank when he killed Howard Kemper.'

Lucy clapped both hands to her mouth. A tight scream issued from between her fingers. Hogan stiffened. Things were getting worse by the second. 'That's awful,' she exclaimed. 'We have a couple of handguns and a shotgun. With all that noise from the storm I never heard a thing. Do you think you can catch him?' Her eyes flicked towards the closet.

'Not a doubt of it. The murdering skunk can't get far. There are search parties out now even as I speak. All the exits from town are covered so we're hopeful of catching the rat before the day is out.' He turned to go. 'Keep a weapon handy and your door locked. This man is dangerous. We also suspect that he robbed the stage. The horses came in last night having been released from their traces. But there was no sign of the coach. Some of the boys have gone out to investigate. Don't worry, we'll catch him. I'll be over with a wagon later to pick up Ezra.'

Lucy closed the door turning to face the suspect. 'Before you say anything,' Hogan blurted out, not having been privy to the hushed conversation

82

upstairs. 'I only shot that lawman because he pulled a gun on me from behind. He'll live. But all that other stuff in the bank wasn't down to me. I was just sheltering there when a lynch mob started chasing after me.'

'If'n you didn't kill Howard Kemper, who did?' The harsh tone of the query was a bleak accusation.

Hogan knew he would have to exert all his persuasive skills to get this girl on his side. 'I don't know. They heard me hiding in the back when I accidently kicked a spittoon. A well dressed guy came rushing out waving his arms. Next thing the fella was gunned down in the back from someone else inside the office.'

'Did you see who it was?'

'I didn't stay to find out.' Hogan's brow furrowed in thought. 'All I know is that a heated disagreement was taking place in there. Whoever pulled the trigger has put the blame squarely on to my shoulders. Now everybody figures I killed this Kemper while trying to rob the bank.' His final comment was a plea for acceptance of his innocence. 'You gotta believe me, ma'am, I had nothing to do with it.' Then something else lurched to the forefront of his mind. 'Who do you think this guy Kemper could have been arguing with to get him shot down like that?'

'It must have been the owner of the bank, Elias Jacoby. He and Kemper were also in business together. The other fellow must have been his guard, Latigo Rennick.'

Lucy's taut expression informed Hogan that their

conjectures were running along mutual lines. He quickly holstered his revolver so as not to frighten her again. 'In that case, my figuring is that Rennick fired the fatal shot. Something must have gone badly wrong with their partnership.' He fixed a beseeching gaze on the girl, silently willing her to believe this version of the grim events. 'Now this snake Jacoby has the whole town believing I'm the culprit.'

Indecision registered in the girl's anxious expression. She moved back a pace, nervously fiddling with her hair, desperate to reach the right conclusion. This man had suddenly invaded her life, and was trying to convince her that the whole town had him tried and convicted. But surely folks she had known her whole life couldn't all be wrong? Nonetheless this man seemed so plausible, so sincere in his denial of the rational deduction – and there could be no denying, he was a strikingly good-looking jasper.

Her elegant features reddened at the notion that such thoughts could be affecting her judgement. The flushed countenance was quickly shrugged off as pragmatism once again took control. She already knew to her cost that Jacoby was a sly, manipulative schemer. His oily suggestion that the loan could be paid off in 'other ways' had displayed that. Her skin crawled at the notion. Perhaps Howard Kemper had uncovered some underhand trickery and threatened to blow the whistle.

But then again, it could all be a charade, weasel words spouted by a killer designed to buy himself time so he could escape the hangman's noose. . . .

Hogan could see that she was not sure of the truth of his contention, but all he could do was allow her to figure things out for herself. And take it from there. No way did he want to force the issue. Neither did he hanker after her wrenching open the door and screaming blue murder. It was a delicate tightrope he was walking.

Then another thought struck him. If, as the medic had said, a deputation had gone to look for the wayward stagecoach, he would be well advised to reveal the grisly details before someone else blurted it out. Unfortunately this thought entered his head too late, and before he could open his mouth, another knock came on the door.

Hogan ducked out of sight as the girl answered the summons. It was Annie Bullock who ran the candy store. 'I'm afraid I've gotten bad news for you, my dear,' she espoused despondently. 'The boys have just returned and they found the stagecoach abandoned near the Devil's Elbow.' The older woman swallowed nervously. 'They found the driver and passengers. . . .' The woman's hesitation was palpable before she added awkwardly, '. . . they'd all been shot dead.'

A cry of anguish erupted from the girl's throat. She clutched at the door frame for support. Mrs Bullock stepped forward, anxious to help ease the pain. 'Do you want me to come in and sit awhile? Your sister was on that coach, wasn't she?' the woman nervously asked.

'Not only her,' Lucy wailed tears streaming down

85

her face. 'She was bringing her daughter Agnes to visit.'

'I'm truly sorry,' the distressed messenger averred laying a comforting arm around the girl's shoulder. 'I'll come in and make you a cup of coffee.'

Lucy was about to concur when her distraught mind kicked back to the reality of her current predicament. Where would it all end? Her whole world was rapidly disintegrating. There was a man no more than six feet away holding a gun that he was prepared to use. Shaking off the deep trauma threatening to engulf her, Lucy thanked the shop keeper for her concern. 'Much obliged for your concern, Annie,' she said, struggling hard to appear grateful, 'but I need some time on my own to take in this dreadful news. You do understand, I hope?'

'Of course, my dear,' Annie replied, patting the girl's arm. 'Any time you want to talk, I'm only across the street.' She stepped down off the porch, adding a parting shot. 'And keep your door locked, honey. There's a killer on the loose and he could be hiding anywhere.'

Lucy nodded, knowing exactly where that hiding place was.

As soon as the door closed behind her, she burst into tears. Hogan stepped forward, taking her in his arms. There was no resistance. She clung to him as the tears flowed. Neither spoke for a long two minutes.

It was Hogan who broke the tense silence. 'I meant to tell you about what I found out there. She beat me to it.' Gently he extricated himself from the girl's clinging grasp. 'Believe me when I say that I'm real sorry for your loss. But it wasn't any of my doing.' The appeal was delivered softly, but with conviction. He lifted her chin, looking deep into those pools of cobalt blue. 'And that's the God's honest truth. I just happened along. Wrong time, wrong place. And now I'm shouldering the blame.'

Lucy took a step back. 'I'll ask you again. And I'll know straightaway should you try lying to me.' She paused before issuing a warning. 'If'n it wasn't you, then who else could have done such a terrible thing?' The heartfelt query was like a slap in the face.

'I can't be sure,' was the measured reply. 'But from what you've told me, I have me a notion that Kemper's shooting and the stage hold-up are somehow linked together. It's too much of a coincidence that they occurred around the same time.'

Outside, the raucous shouts of men calling to each other could be heard drawing ever closer. 'The doc said they were organizing a house-to-house search this morning. You're gonna have to make up your mind, ma'am.' He removed the heavy .44 Remington from his holster and handed it to her. 'If you figure I'm the killer, then let them arrest me. I'm in your hands now.' Hogan knew he was taking a huge risk by adopting this ploy. But he was gambling on the logic of his appeal, and that his apparent surrender would register positively with the girl.

He walked into the kitchen and poured two cups of coffee from the steaming pot, then sat down at the table. Handing one to Lucy, he took a sip and fixed her with a beseeching look – neither a frown nor a smile, just an open entreaty to reach the right decision. Lucy put the gun down on the table and turned away, sipping the coffee while she mulled over what he had said. A movement above served to remind her of the other problem that was looming with her father's future – though all she could do there was trust in the skill of Doc Barnett.

As for her immediate dilemma, could it really be the case that Elias Jacoby was behind the robbery? She knew this particular stage had been carrying a strongbox as well as passengers. The more she thought about it, the more suspicious she became. If this man was telling the truth, the banker must have sanctioned the killing of his partner by Rennick.

Hogan appeared to read her thoughts. He pressed home his case further. 'It stands to reason. Kemper was running scared after he heard about the killings and threatened to pull out of the deal. Jacoby had him shot to save his own skin. Don't that make sense to you?' He was warming to this chance of swaying the girl in his favour. 'And then he claimed it was *me* shot his pard and tried to rob the bank. My guess is that he organized the stage robbery. And me happening along by accident was an excuse to throw the blame elsewhere.'

The logic of his argument, not to mention this man's sincerity, found Lucy Courtright grudgingly accepting his explanation. She sat down. 'You can't stay here,' she said. 'Sooner or later they'll want to search the house. I can put them off for the time being, claiming Pa needs to sleep. But only for a day.'

'That's all right, ma'am. I'll wait until dark, then try to sneak past the guards they've posted.' But Hogan could see by the fear showing in her tense gaze that she was still not fully convinced of his innocence. He had broken into her home brandishing a gun, with the whole town searching for him. Could he blame her?

'Before you go, I figure you owe me some kind of explanation. Just appearing out of nowhere and claiming you have been set up is hard to swallow.' The girl's demand was delivered in a calm yet blunt manner. 'And it better be good. I'm not a woman to be crossed or made a fool of.' Her flinty expression left the intruder in no doubt of the consequences should his explanation be less than adequate.

'It's a long story,' Hogan sighed. 'Reckon I'd better introduce myself afore I begin. The name is Deke Hogan, ex-major recently with the Confederate army.' He paused allowing the introduction to sink in, hoping the girl would mellow. But she remained stubbornly tight-lipped. 'Maybe you could brew us a fresh pot of coffee before I start. And some of those cinnamon cookies I spotted would help loosen my tongue as well.'

The endearing smile aimed at easing the tension enveloping the two unlikely associates was curtly brushed aside. Qualms of uncertainty had dissipated Lucy's burgeoning warmth of acceptance. Nevertheless, she stood up and busied herself in the kitchen while Hogan prepared his story.

Once settled with coffee and cookies, he outlined in full the events that had led to his current predicament. The only thing left out was the unedifying episode in Tucumcari. Even he recognized that revelation would be a step too far. The narrator finished his tale by firmly assuring the girl that he had happened across the stagecoach by accident after he and his gang had split up to go their separate ways after learning that the war was over.

It was a story that could not have been concocted on the spur of the moment. That much Lucy was forced to acknowledge once he had finished. Surely nobody could have invented such a bizarre train of events. They both sat on opposite sides of the table, sipping their coffee and munching on the cookies. It had been a lot for the girl to absorb.

Hogan was now eager to ascertain where he stood in this woman's estimation. Did she believe him? Or was he about to be hung out to dry? An unfortunate choice of words on which to reflect.

The Remington was lying where she had left it, a potent symbol of death that had invaded her simple life. Slowly her hand reached across and grasped the steely blue of the barrel, and handed it back to the owner.

Hogan breathed a deep sigh of relief.

'So what happens now?' she finally enquired. For the first time, a coy smile played across her features, promise of a dazzling radiance brighter than a full moon. But it was only momentary, replaced by a frown of anxiety. 'Stay here much longer and you're bound to be discovered. My name is Lucy Courtright, by the way.'

Hogan resisted the temptation to deliver the trite phrase as to what a lovely name it was. Instead he got down to the business of extricating them both from this disquieting relationship. 'As I said before, it's best I stay here until nightfall, then leave.' He paused to embrace her with a wishful gaze. 'Hopefully you'll never have to set eyes on me again.' In truth that was the last thing he wanted. But the bleak winds of destiny had chosen otherwise. And they both knew it. 'Maybe you could have a look out there and see what's going on, and with a bit of luck get me the lowdown on how to quit this town in one piece.'

She nodded, unfastening her apron before donning a coat and hat. 'While I'm out it would be best if'n you stayed down in the cellar. Just in case they come by and decide to search the place in my absence. I'll keep the cellar door locked.'

TEN

DARK SIDE OF THE MOON

Lucy was gone for some time, though how long it was impossible to determine. All Hogan could do was wait it out in the cellar, pacing up and down watching as the light slowly faded. Eventually movement above heralded her return. Then he heard voices. The gun leapt into his hand, body muscles tightening. A heavy silence followed. It seemed an age before the bolt on the cellar door slid back. Hogan stood ready to defend himself, but then the girl's swirling blue dress appeared and he gave a gasp of relief.

'That was Doc Barnett and his assistant taking Pa to the surgery.' He followed her back upstairs. Blotchy cheeks informed Hogan that she had been crying. 'They've brought the bodies back in coffins

92

and placed them inside the church along with Howard Kemper ready for an all-night vigil.' More tears followed. 'Elias Jacoby has said he will take the first two hour watch. The funeral and burials are to take place tomorrow afternoon.'

Hogan didn't want to rush her, but he was anxious to learn about the town 'vigil' being kept for him. Where were the guards posted? Knowing the importance of her reconnaissance, Lucy didn't keep him waiting. 'Jacoby made it plain there will be no relaxation of the hunt to find you. Glory Be has been shut down tighter than a bank vault. I don't know how you're going to escape.'

'I'll figure a way out. There's always a loophole that's been overlooked. And I mean to find it.' They stood facing one another, both feeling awkward, not quite knowing how to say goodbye. It was left to Hogan to make the first move. Sheepishly he removed his billfold and peeled off a couple of notes. 'It's the least I can do to repay your help,' he said.

Straightaway he knew he had done the wrong thing as Lucy spurned the offer, pushing it away. 'I don't want your money. I did this because I think you've been wrongly blamed for this tragedy. No amount of money can bring those folks back. Now that I know what kind of man Elias Jacoby is, I'll do my darndest to make him pay for his crimes.'

Hogan took her in his arms. A warm kiss was planted on her upturned mouth. There was no resistance as they clung together. Neither wanted the tender moment to end. But end it must. Stay and he

93

was a doomed man for sure.

'One day I'll come back and help you dig out the proof needed to net the real culprits. And then perhaps . . .' He left the sentence unfinished. Both of them knew the reality of their circumstances had chosen otherwise. Their lives were heading along divergent trails. A final kiss on the forehead and he slipped out of the back door. A raised hand and he was gone.

All she could do now was pray for this man to make a safe getaway – this enigmatic stranger who had suddenly entered her life, and just as quickly departed. It was almost as if he had never existed. Then his handsome face swam into her mind and she knew it had been all too real. Tears once again coursed down her cheeks.

Deke Hogan was totally unaware of the passions he had left behind as he paused at the corner of the store. Anxiously he watched as a passing cloud toyed with the bright orb of the moon, which was bathing the town in its ethereal glow. Too slowly the cloud slid across the surface, laughing at the witness to its mischievous game. Then with a final shrug it surrendered, and darkness shrouded the town below.

Moving like a ghostly wraith, Hogan made his way towards the church, its tower poking above the rest of the town. Flitting through the shadows in this way was known territory to him, reminiscent of the shadowy world of covert espionage he had perfected over the last four years. As such he easily managed to avoid any undesirable encounters.

Only after he had left the relative safety of the saddle store did he make the decision to confront the treacherous banker. From what Lucy had said, the skunk would be alone inside the church, ostensibly grieving over his dead friend. Hogan ground his teeth in anger. The devious varmint had hoodwinked the whole darned town. He might not be able to change their minds, but he could exact a fitting retribution of his own.

First, though, he needed to check the positions of the guards posted to prevent his escape. They had no idea what he looked like, which meant that every stranger leaving Glory Be would be stopped and questioned. By the time he reached the outer limits of the town, numerous escape routes had been spotted. Even those being patrolled held little in the way of a threat.

The sentinels had become less than alert. Failure to capture the fugitive had sapped their initial enthusiasm. With his hat pulled down, Hogan chuckled to himself. He even passed the time of day with one group, asking if they had had any luck. The despondent response cheered him no end. 'Not yet, but the critter won't get past us, eh boys?' Jaded grunts of accord emerged from the other guards, all of whom displayed a noteworthy lack of zeal. Escape from this burg would be a breeze. They had even left horses tethered inside a nearby corral.

Satisfied that his departure would be simply achieved, he returned to the church, sliding round its solid bulk, feeling his way towards the rear. The

95

door opened to his touch without a sound, which might have betrayed his presence. The glow of candles offered sufficient light to guide him into the main body of the church.

And there were the coffins, lined up as if on parade – which perhaps they were – awaiting God's blessing. Each had a wreath of flowers, except for the last one, which was smaller than the others, with the doll he remembered perched atop. A lump formed in the fugitive's throat.

Jacoby was casually smoking a cigar, an oily smirk on his face made all the more subversive by the flickering glimmer of the candles. A growl of anger was forcibly suppressed by the watcher girding himself for the confrontation.

Outside the wind had blown up again. Its eerie chorus sifted through the many nooks and crannies imbuing a macabre elegy of death stirring the shadows into motion. Hogan shivered. Just so long as it isn't my demise, he mused. The noise had deadened his approach.

But the sentinel had sensed a presence and jerked round. 'Who's there?' came the jittery response. 'Show yourself.'

'Over here!' The blunt reply saw Jacoby spinning on his heel as a dark silhouette emerged from the gloom. Without uttering a word, the blurred image soon became more resolved, and Deke Hogan moved slowly forwards. 'Guess you know who I am,' the wronged man hissed. The stiff posture, uncompromising, chock full of menace, hovered beside the child's coffin like a predatory eagle. He reached out and delicately touched the doll, a critical eye scrutinizing his adversary and making no attempt to hide his contempt.

So this was the loathsome toad who had caused him all the trouble. What he perceived was a noxious individual running to fat in all the wrong places, no doubt due to good living at the expense of innocent contributors forced to pay inflated rents, in addition to the illicit loot from robberies. The natty blue suit and frilly silk shirt were enhanced by a diamond stick pin securing a black neck-tie. A waxed moustache and goatee beard only added to the odious persona of a leech on the take.

'I've never set eyes on you before. What are you doing here?' Jacoby declared, ardently wishing Latigo Rennick would arrive early for his shift. A catch in the man's throat betrayed his apprehension. 'This is a private affair, a vigil in memory of friends and fellow citizens before their funeral tomorrow.'

'You know exactly who I am. More to the point, you know why I'm here.'

'I have no idea who you are,' Jacoby protested. But his denial sounded hollow, deceitful and two-faced. 'What business can I possibly have with a stranger?'

Hogan smiled before answering. 'The business of answering for the crimes of robbery and murder that you committed and heaped on to my shoulders, Mister Elias Jacoby.' He gently tapped the coffin, the macabre sound echoing around the stone vaulted nave. 'You're nothing but a conniving skunk and a backshooter.' The blunt accusation was punched out with venom.

The banker gulped, looking round for the help that wasn't there. 'I d-don't know y-you,' he jabbered stepping back. 'You must be mistaken . . .'

'Don't deny it,' Hogan rasped, butting in. 'I was there, remember, when your partner was shot in the back. And now I'm gonna make you pay for throwing the blame on me.' Hogan hunkered down into the classic gunfighter's stance, his right hand flexing above the gun butt. 'You've gotten this whole town believing your lies, and all I can do is cut off the snake's head. It might not prove my innocence, but it'll sure make *me* feel a whole lot better. Now get to shooting, big shot!' He was confident that a couple of shots would not penetrate the thick walls and betray his presence.

'But I ain't carrying,' the braggart pleaded. 'You can't shoot an unarmed man.' He lifted the edges of his jacket to prove the point.

Hogan hawked out a brittle laugh, totally lacking any hint of mirth. 'It figures,' he sneered. 'Lowlife critters like you always get other suckers to do their dirty work. Well, they ain't here to watch your back.'

Desperation found the banker pleading for his life with the only other thing he valued. 'Listen to me. I'm willing to share the proceeds with you if'n you turn around and disappear from Glory Be. Fifty-fifty, that's ten thousand bucks. So what do you say? Is it a deal?'

Hogan's contemptuous response was to spit on the

floor. Not another word was uttered as he stepped forward and slapped the crook in the face. Jacoby staggered back, clutching at the altar to stop himself falling over. 'I ain't no dirty crook like you. And there are other ways to gain satisfaction.'

Without any preamble, he launched himself at the varmint, catching him with a solid right, high on the head. His left hand grabbed the rat's shirt. Buttons popped, a rending of cloth echoing around the sanctuary. Another right aimed at the jutting chin was blocked as Jacoby hung on. Both men went down, rolling across the dirt floor. The banker was the first to scramble to his feet. A heavy boot found its way into Hogan's stomach.

Elias Jacoby was no pushover. He might have softened up in recent years, but a ruthless streak attained in his early years as an enforcer for numerous land agents had bred a tough skin. Only later when the message finally clicked that all the wealth was in the hands of bankers, did he set up on his own. Blackmail and extortion of gullible partners, allied to a sharp intellect, enabled him to hoodwink them, providing the trickster with the necessary capital.

Acute trepidation at losing everything now lent fire to his retaliation. The killer was damned if this interfering firebrand was going to spoil the profitable racket he had established here in Glory Be. Another brutal kick was deflected, enabling Hogan to scuttle crabwise out of reach. Jacoby snarled, grabbing hold of a heavy brass candlestick. 'You won't leave here alive, mister,' he rasped, springing forwards with the brutal instrument raised for the killing blow.

As the crook loomed over him, Hogan waited till the last second before rolling sideways. The candlestick missed his head by a whisker and clanged on the floor, forcing Jacoby to let go and throwing him off balance. The more agile Hogan leapt to his feet, carrying the fight back to his assailant.

Back and forth they swayed, trading blows and upending vases of flowers. Each of the protagonists had sustained cut lips and bruises, but Hogan was gaining the upper hand. Stepping back to avoid a swinging haymaker, a straight left to Jacoby's jaw connected with stunning force, flooring the burly crook.

Straightaway Hogan was on him – but just as his fist lifted to deliver the *coup de grace* their eyes met, and Hogan perceived that Jacoby's panic-stricken gawp had shifted to something behind his attacker's left shoulder. A momentary flicker of movement reflected in the wide-eyed look was all Hogan needed to figure the grim truth.

He immediately threw himself to one side, swivelling in a single fluid motion and drawing his revolver. Nevada Bass Tiptree had been just about to lay his gun barrel across Hogan's exposed head, but now found himself outsmarted, two bullets plugging him in the guts.

But the tussle wasn't over: Latigo had been standing by the front door when the encounter with Tiptree started, and seeing his buddy cut down, he aimed a couple of shots at the killer – but the distance was too long for handgun accuracy and the bullets went wide, chipping hunks of stone from a nearby pillar.

Outside, the wind had lifted to a howling chorus as if cheering on the combatants. With bullets flying every which way inside the building, Jacoby took the opportunity to conceal himself behind the altar. Hogan scrambled across the floor to the edge of the far aisle. Slowly, and with gun held at the ready, he began crawling along the line of seats, pausing behind the next pillar. A quick glance informed his searching gaze that the other gunman was creeping up the adjoining aisle.

Light from a candle glinted off the Manhattan clutched in his hand. One of these bad guys had killed Howard Kemper, and there was no way he was going to sit back and allow the same thing to happen here. He waited until Latigo had passed his position, moving cautiously towards the altar.

Then he stood up calling for the owlhooter to surrender. It had always been his position to give an opponent the chance to call it quits. 'The game's up, mister,' he snapped out. The growled command bounced off the stone adobe walls of the church. 'Throw down that hogleg, you're covered.'

Rennick wasn't slow in responding to the challenge, and both his weapons spat fire and hot lead at one and the same time. But the outlaw's shot was hurried, unlike Hogan's, which lifted the guy's hat and scored a furrow across his scalp. Rennick fell to the ground moaning. With one man dead in the blink of an eye and the other wounded, panic gripped the unnerved banker, who hollered at the top of his voice for assistance.

He needn't have bothered. His two bodyguards had left the front door of the church wide open, and the raucous blast of gunfire had awakened the lethargic torpor of the sentinels, who now came running from different directions. 'What's all the shooting about?' a nervous voice shouted through a broken window near the door. Nobody entered the church, fear clamping their innards in its vice-like grip.

'The killer's in here and he's shot down both my guards in cold blood,' Jacoby replied, still lurking in fear behind the altar. 'He needs to be caught before anyone else is hurt.' He was thinking specifically of his own miserable hide.

Hogan knew that his position inside the church was extremely vulnerable. Outside the main door firebrands illuminated the milling throng, who were shuffling nervously, unsure what to do next. Pretty soon they would figure out that surrounding the building was the best way of securing their prey.

Escape was now essential if the fugitive was to remain at liberty. Regrets for having made the decision to confront the black-hearted banker were futile. The foolhardy act of bravado had backfired, revitalizing the crowd and making it that much tougher to effect an escape.

He hustled back the way he had come, making his exit by the side door. His adversary's palpable alarm as he retreated presented Jacoby with the courage to further urge the credulous multitude to decisive action: 'He's getting away out back, men,' came the confident assertion. 'Spread out and catch the bastard! I'll double the bonus for the man that brings him in, dead or alive.'

For Deke Hogan every second counted. As he left the church, a clutch of pursuers appeared at the corner of the building. 'There he goes!' hollered Sowbelly, leading the chase. Bullets tracked the fleeting shadow fading into the Stygian gloom. Fear of being captured and its blatant aftermath lent wings to his flight. For the moment all he wanted was to put some distance behind him.

Dodging this way and that among the chaotic array of makeshift hutments that had attached themselves to the growing settlement, desperation made him curse his crazy lack of judgement. He could have been well on his way by now, heading back home. Now he was back to square one. Yet deep down he knew that leaving Glory Be was never going to be an option. He had to stay and clear his name.

That notion told him there was only one place where he would be safe. At every sound of the approaching pursuit he was forced to hunker down until the danger passed. Now he knew exactly what the wild deer that he had once stalked back in the Big Piney woodlands of Missouri felt like: stop and start, this way and that – all the while listening, teasing out alien sounds. It was not a pleasant sentiment. Patience had to override snatched decisions. Slowly and with extreme care he managed to steer a course back to the rear of the saddle store.

Once again he raised the trap door and slipped down into the cellar. There he slumped down on to the familiar blankets. But there could be no rest until he had made his presence known to Lucy Courtright. And how would she react to his sudden and unexpected reappearance?

ELEVEN

TROJAN HORSE

Elias Jacoby was badly shaken up when he finally emerged from the church. Fear gripped him in a tight embrace – fear that this illusive will-o'-the-wisp would continue to play games with his pursuers and would be waiting to gun him down when he showed his face. It was a disquieting, if not scary notion. With Tiptree dead and Latigo wounded, he was in a weak position. Easing his bulky frame out of the church door, he was met with darkness thick as treacle. At least the billowing clouds of wind-blown sand made him a hazy, obscure target.

Beady eyes flicked back and forth as he hustled along the boardwalk, anxious to reach the protection of Windy Wilf's saloon. And once there he intended staying in his personal quarters until this jasper was caught. But first, he needed a bottle of Scotch to calm his jangled nerves.

With some measure of self-belief restored, he summoned an emergency meeting of the town council to meet in Windy Wilf's. Confidence was soon further restored when friends and colleagues arrived, and a rejuvenated Elias Jacoby resolved to maintain his own interpretation of justice. Gone was the quaking lily-livered wretch who had come face to face with the grim reaper inside the church. He stood to address them, back ramrod straight, a grim countenance enfolding the gathering of lackeys. Clearly they had not run the quarry to ground.

This guy was becoming a perilous distraction – and then another thought caused his overstuffed face to blanch, namely the illusive jackal might even have escaped, skipped town altogether and be heading who knows where. And once he reached the nearest town, the whole damned mess would be out in the open. If indeed that was the case, there was only one sure way of tracking the varmint down.

'Arnold!' he called across to the coaching agent. 'Go get Inky Jaxx and tell him to come over here lickety split.' Christened Indigo, Jaxx had earned the nickname due to his permanently black fingers. He was the local editor in charge of the weekly news sheet, a two-page rag affiliated to the more widespread *San Isobel Courier*.

Arnold Tasker knew better than to grumble at the brusque command. Jacoby was still leader of the council with the power to back his actions. Ten minutes later the newsman appeared, looking even more ink-stained than usual. The murders were big news for a small town like Glory Be. Good reports distributed through the *Courier* could make his name, with the chance to quit this one-horse dump for a more prestigious job in the big city.

He was none too pleased at being dragged away from his vital preparations. 'Something you want?' he grunted, wiping a blackened paw across his face. 'I'm a busy man with all this hoo-ha going on.'

Jacoby silenced the bluster with a withering glare. 'They tell me you're a good pen artist as well as a news hound. That true?' he snapped out.

The assertion certainly caught the editor's attention. 'None better, Mr Jacoby,' he replied in a somewhat chastened manner.

'Well, listen up good. I got a good look at this killer that's terrorizing our town. I want you to do me an accurate drawing and have it circulated throughout the territory as soon as possible. Reckon you can do that?' He quickly sweetened the demand by offering a substantial monetary inducement. 'That skunk could have quit town already. I want him caught and brought back here to face justice – better still, over a saddle. Make sure you offer a reward of two thousand dollars. It will be payable from my own personal account.'

With wide eyes Inky stuttered a reply to the affirmative. 'I'll get on to it straightaway, sir. You can count on me. One of my express riders can deliver it to the *Courier* office in Salida by riding all day and night non-stop.'

Jacoby responded with a haughty nod as if he

expected nothing less. 'The rest of you can organize a house-to-house search starting at first light. If'n he's still skulking around here I want the skunk dug out. And nobody will blame any of you for shooting him down on sight.'

He waved an arm, arrogantly dismissing the shuffling assemblage – all apart from one man, whom he beckoned across to join him at the bar. Pouring a drink of best Scotch, he pushed it towards the frowning Sowbelly Clover. The pig farmer eyed the drink nervously, wondering what he had done to merit such a reward from a bigwig like Jacoby. 'Drink up, Sowbelly. I have a proposition for you.'

The artless simpleton sipped his drink, waiting for the disclosure. His tongue lapped across his lips – it sure was good liquor. Jacoby struggled to conceal his distaste at the rank odour emanating from the pig man: the numbskull's shabby appearance was in total contrast to the banker's urbane persona. That said, he was the ideal patsy to assist Jacoby in retaining his grip on the town.

'How would you feel about taking on the role of acting marshal while poor old Ike Stanford is laid up?' He placed the revered star on the counter. 'Do a solid job and perhaps it could become a permanent position. There's good pay for the right man. And I need someone I can trust implicitly.'

Clover was stunned. Nobody had ever considered him for anything more than raising pigs and making up a foursome at poker. Suddenly being offered the chance to attain the prestigious height of town marshal was beyond his wildest dreams. A distinct feather in his cap. The star winked at him as if to say, come and get me. Sowbelly did not need a second bidding.

'You got yourself a deal, Mr Jacoby sir,' he asserted, gleefully picking up the star and pinning it to his chest. 'I'll sure do my darndest to bring this fella in.'

'Then get to it . . . marshal,' the banker replied, barely able to conceal a derisive smirk. 'And remember, that reward of two thousand goes to the man who captures this critter.' He winked at the ingenuous oaf. 'Preferably dead, eh?'

Jacoby felt like his old self. With mooncalves such as Jaxx and Clover in his pocket, the future was looking much brighter. He rubbed his hands. 'Set 'em up, Windy. I reckon we both deserve a drink.'

The saloon manager was less optimistic, although he concealed his reservations. This ghostly killer was still on the loose, and until he was caught there was no telling how things would pan out.

Even in the dark, Hogan could have found his way up into the main body of the saddle shop. All he had to do was avoid the hanging haunches of pork, the table, spare saddles and tack over to his left, then through into the next room. Thankfully the puppies were still absent. The wooden flight of stairs was on the far side. Eight steps and he had reached the door.

Here he paused, listening intently for any movement. It was still early. Would Lucy be up and about? Had she managed to shut out the deep traumas of the previous days to earn a decent sleep – unlike her hidden guest, who had tossed and turned for most of the night? He desperately needed the boost of strong coffee to maintain his vigilance. Following the previous night's gun battle, Jacoby would leave no stone unturned in his search for the killer of his bodyguard.

Hogan felt dirtied, fouled by having been forced down to the braggart's level. Now they really could accuse him of murder, and it made no difference that he had only been defending himself. And sooner or later they would come here and insist on delving into every cupboard and closet. He had to leave so as not to place Lucy in the impossible position of having to choose. This was her town. He was merely a passing drifter, a stranger who had blundered into her life.

Gently he pushed open the door and stepped into the main body of the shop. And there she was, arranging some stirrups on a shelf with her back to him. He coughed gently so as not to alarm her. Immediately she spun round, a hand reaching for a nearby handgun. For a moment they both stood facing one another, unsure what to say. It was the girl who broke the awkward silence: 'I heard all the shooting last night and figured they must have caught you. Or even. . . .' She gulped, unable to finish.

'They would have as well if'n I hadn't managed to evade them and come here.' Without waiting for a reply he hurried on: 'But I won't stay. All I need is

110

some vittles and a pot of coffee to see me on my way. Then I won't be bothering you no more. I'm truly sorry for the mess I've brought down on your head.'

Even as they were speaking, the ominous sound of the early morning search penetrated the adobe walls of the store. Lucy hustled across to the main window.

'They're out already,' she said as Hogan joined her. Groups of men were on both side of the street, while others had disappeared along side roads. The hunt was on with a vengeance. In a surprisingly calm voice, Lucy addressed the dilemma in a lucid and forthright manner. 'I figure they won't reach this end of town for another two hours. That gives us enough time to get you away.'

Employment of the word 'us' made Hogan's heart leap. But how could she possible help him evade these voracious hunters? 'You don't have to do this,' he asserted firmly. 'I don't want to cause you any more trouble. Especially since I had to kill one of Jacoby's men who tried to ambush me in the church.' Lucy's eyes lifted, but her face did not betray the slightest hint of condemnation. 'Best I just sneak out now and take my chances.'

Lucy held up a hand. Determination showed in her whole demeanour, the set of her shoulders. Here was a woman not to be swayed from her resolve. Her mind was made up. 'I know now you wouldn't have done that without just cause. We have enough time for breakfast. Then we can put into action the plan I have in mind.'

Over a meal of bacon, eggs and fried potatoes

washed down with a gallon of Arbuckles finest, Hogan explained what had occurred the previous night and how it had all gone haywire. The meal certainly boosted his brain as well as his weary body. Now he was ready to face anything that was tossed his way.

Lucy's plan to effect his escape had come to mind because she had recently read about the defeat of the Trojans, made famous in ancient Greek legend. Now she intended to pull off the same stunt in reverse. To this end the store wagon was brought round from the livery stable where it was kept, and parked at the back of the house. Hogan waited on tenterhooks, nervously watching through the front window as the searchers drew ever closer. On hearing the rattle of the wagon out back, he breathed a sigh of relief, carefully peering out of the rear window to ensure the coast was clear. Before leaving, Lucy pinned a note on to the front door stating the saddle store was closed temporarily due to illness.

As arranged, Hogan scrambled into the bed of the wagon, concealing himself inside a large wooden crate just big enough for a man to lie in. Lucy put the lid over him, nailing it down. He flinched. Inside it felt like being in a coffin. He prayed silently this would not become its prime purpose. The hairs on the back of his neck prickled in recollection of a similar tight spot when the support palings of a trench had collapsed under shellfire at Chancellorsville. He and Charlie Bone had been forced to lie there while the enemy pounded by overhead. Only when the light faded were they able to crawl away to safety. Hogan emerged unscathed, unlike Charlie, who lost an eye. This was not quite the same, but he still needed to clamp his eyes shut to combat the nausea threatening to bubble over.

Thankfully the wagon soon lumbered into motion. All Hogan could do now was trust that this particular Trojan would pull the same trick as his ancient counterparts. Hogan could hear the girl calling to passersby that she was collecting her father to take him back to their holding in Lodge Pole Canyon. True enough. What she did not reveal was that there would be an additional passenger.

When the wagon stopped at the surgery, Doc Barnett helped the injured man into the bed of the wagon. 'I'm sure sorry I couldn't save your leg, Ezra. You'll need to adapt a stirrup to accommodate the wooden replacement when the wound has healed. I'll be round next week to fit the new one.'

The old timer grunted. 'No darned pegleg is gonna keep me out the saddle.'

Barnett wagged an admonitory finger at him. 'But no bronc busting. That's an order. You try that again and you'll likely lose the other leg as well.' More huffing and puffing.

Lucy added her firm support to that of the medic. 'You heard the doctor, Pa,' she maintained. 'And you might as well know now that I've hired a new man to help out while you're recovering.' Further protestations were ignored as she cracked the whip to get the team moving. 'And I'm going to make sure you toe

113

the line.' Hogan smiled, but couldn't help wondering what Courtright's reaction would be had he known his daughter was assisting a wanted man lying adjacent to him.

Head held high she headed down the main street, cautiously noting the various search parties entering stores and houses. But nobody gave her a second thought. Just another wagon going about its lawful business. Lying prone without moving was frustrating to the fugitive, not least because his muscles were tightening up with cramp. All he could do was bite back the pain.

But once they had ridden well beyond the town limits Lucy pulled into a side draw behind some rocks. 'What we stopping for, gal?' her pa hawked out.

'You'll see,' she averred, a sly grin creasing the sylph-like features. Swinging a leg over the back rest, she stepped into the bed of the wagon and began levering up the securing nails from the crate.

All Ezra could manage was a wide-eyed stare, unable to comprehend his daughter's odd behaviour. When she raised the lid, he received the surprise of his life. There, as if rising from the dead, a man's head appeared, followed by a lean-limbed frame stretching the stiffness from his muscles.

'Boy!' the ghost ejaculated. 'Am I glad to be out of that coffin!'

That was the moment Ezra found his voice. 'What in thunderation?' he exclaimed, his eyes on stalks. 'You trying to succeed where that sawbones failed

114

and give me a heart attack, gal?'

Hogan offered the startled oldtimer a broad smile of greeting, holding out a hand. 'Pleased to meet you, Mr Courtright,' he said, as the stunned rancher accepted the proffered appendage. 'The name is Deke Hogan. It appears that I'm your new hand.'

The following ten minutes were spent explaining the grim nature of the subterfuge that Hogan and his daughter had been forced to organize. 'So let's get this straight,' the old timer declared, still unable to comprehend the dubious story he had just been told. 'You're certain that Jacoby killed his partner, but he claimed that you did it while trying to rob the bank. And then he persuaded the whole town that you were responsible for robbing the stage and killing all the passengers.'

'I know it all sounds mighty far-fetched, Mr Courtright,' Hogan asserted. 'But it's the goldarned truth. And the only way I could prove my innocence was by getting Jacoby to confess his involvement. But that was scotched when his men turned up at the church.' He then pulled out the silver concho and showed it to the horse trader. 'This is my only hope now. It was snatched by one of the victims. If I can find out who it belongs to I'll have my proof.'

The old guy's leathery face was scrunched in thought as he studied the unusual piece of evidence. He scratched his head. 'I've seen that design before some place. But I just can't bring it to mind. It'll come to me in time. Let's hope it will be sooner rather than later.'

With Courtright persuaded that his surprise wagon guest was on the level, Hogan felt that maybe at last the tide had turned in his favour. He scrambled on to the bench seat with Lucy and set the team in motion. It was a two-hour drive to Lodge Pole Canyon. Hogan's first sighting of the homestead brought a lump to the ex-military man's throat.

Memories of a home he had not visited in four years came flooding back. The wooden shack with its stone chimney breast, a hay barn to one side and fields of growing crops. And there was even an orchard. Closer inspection revealed his favourite fruit – peaches.

He drew the wagon to a halt. The wistful expression was noted by the girl, who touched his arm. 'I know what you're thinking,' she whispered in his ear, low enough for her father not to hear. 'And I won't stand in your way.'

Deke nodded, offering Lucy a sad smile. Both of them knew that he would at some point be heading back east to Missouri. A promise he had made to return was left hanging in the air. Much depended on what happened in Glory Be and how he was going to clear his name and bring the true culprits to justice. He nudged the team back into motion. A brooding silence descended over the wagon as it trundled towards Deke's new, if temporary refuge.

TWELVE

LODGE POLE

The next few days were spent familiarizing himself with the working of the spread. It was much the same as what he had been used to before the war. Only the crops were different – squash, pumpkins and maize as against cotton. With such a delectable guide to explain the various tasks, it was an idyllic period, marred only by the unsettling circumstances that could not be ignored. But even after such a short period, Hagan could see the potential for expanding the place.

Horses were not his area of expertise, but he had worked the family farm since taking his first steps guiding the plough horse alongside his pa. And just like the elder Hogan, he figured that if he were to stay around at Lodge Pole, his aim would be to construct a dam, thus capturing the winter rains against when the drought came.

In the evenings old Ezra delighted in regaling his new hand with tales of daring-do in his younger days as a gold prospector, buffalo hunter and bronc buster. And they always ended with him insisting that pretty soon he would be back in the saddle ready to round up a fresh herd of wild mustangs. The obvious hindrance of a peg-leg was ignored.

Lucy busied herself looking after her father when Doc Barnett unexpectedly called to check on his patient. Hogan made himself scarce. No sense in tempting fate. News that a pen drawing of the alleged killer provided by Elias Jacoby's detailed description had been circulated far and wide came as a shock. But so long as he kept his head down he considered it ought not to cause any problems. Though for how long he could keep that up was now in the lap of the gods.

On the fifth day, Lucy announced that she would be going to town for fresh supplies and to check on the store. In truth she was going to call upon the banker to plead for extra time to repay the outstanding loan. Even though the crooked rat was head of the Land Agency, he was still responsible to a board of directors. His criminal activities had no bearing on the legality of the agreed loan.

The three of them were sat round the table on the veranda having a bite to eat after a hard morning's work, for Hogan at least. Ezra Courtright had been more than happy to sit in his favourite rocking chair on the porch, smoking a cigar while directing operations. He might have lost his mobility, but there was nothing wrong with his eyes. 'We've gotten us a visitor,' he muttered leaning forward crinkling his wizened face and squinting to identify the newcomer. 'What in tarnation is old Sowbelly doing out here?' he posited.

Hogan immediately disappeared inside the cabin. The other two stood up awaiting the arrival of the pig farmer. It was Ezra who posed the obvious question as he hauled rein. And it was voiced in a less than welcoming manner when he spotted the tin star pinned to the guy's vest. 'You seem to have come up in the world, Sowbelly. So what can we do for you?' The new lawman appeared somewhat reluctant to state his business. 'Come on, out with it,' Ezra snorted impatiently.

Sowbelly swallowed nervously, handing over an envelope. 'I've been given this job while Ike Stanford is erm . . . indisposed. Mr Jacoby told me to give you this, seeing as he represents the interests of the Land Agency.'

Ezra breathed out a deep sigh, handing it to his daughter. 'You best read this, girl. My letters ain't so good these days.' In truth he had never learned to read more than news headlines. Lucy's eyes widened in shock as the import of the missive struck home. 'What does it say?' her father asked, an edgy rasp betraying his trepidation.

'He can't do this,' she protested vehemently. 'Seven days to repay the full loan or the land will be repossessed? It ain't right. You tell that charlatan we need more time. We were told on signing the contract that three months' notice would be given for the final repayment.'

A shrug of the shoulders was the tin star's response. 'Don't blame me, Lucy. I'm just the messenger,' was the contrite apology. 'But Jacoby was adamant. Said he had the backing of the entire board. There won't be no extension granted. According to him you should have read the small print. Sorry folks, but there it is.' Without waiting for a reply, he swung his horse around and galloped off, relieved that the unwholesome chore was over.

'What are we going to do?' Lucy mumbled, her shoulders drooping with anguish. 'We don't have one hundred dollars, let alone three thousand.'

Hogan rejoined them once their visitor was out of sight. He was visibly stunned by this demand from the banker. No intimation had come his way that Lucy and her father were being hassled by Jacoby. Obscure yet binding clauses were often concealed in contracts enacted by dubious bodies. That was one good reason among many for hiring a lawyer to go over it with a fine tooth comb. Unfortunately, Ezra Courtright had been in too much of a hurry to set up in the horse-breaking business to consider such a vital necessity.

Now the omission was rebounding on him with a vengeance. The old man was full of remorse. But that didn't pay the bill. Hogan stood up and paced along the veranda, his mind mulling over the obvious solution. Wasn't this girl and her father worthy of his help? After all, it was only three thousand dollars.

There would still be plenty left to help out back home.

'There is one way to scupper Jacoby's plan to gain possession of the spread,' he said, in a quietly measured cadence. Both Ezra and his daughter looked at their new hand, uncertainty and disbelief conveyed across their ashen features. 'I could give you the money.'

It was Lucy who recovered her voice first. 'Maybe you would like to explain, Deke. Three thousand is a heap of dough. Far more than any normal guy could have in his possession – unless. . . .' The intimation, implicit yet unstated, was clear as the ice-capped Crestone Peak at the head of Lodge Pole Canyon. Ezra was likewise eager to discover the origin of this sudden windfall. Although he was much less likely to question the ethics inherent in its acquisition. Paying off the debt and keeping the ranch were his prime concerns.

Hogan's interjection was direct, an unequivocal denial of the obvious. 'It ain't what you think,' he professed. 'This dough did not come off that stagecoach. Like I said before, I'm certain Jacoby and his cronies are behind that.'

'Then perhaps you need to clarify exactly where it did come from. And please, no lies. I want the truth.' Her words were firm and direct, delivered with blunt firmness.

Hogan knew there was no riding around this obstacle. Lucy Courtright was astute enough to spot any attempt he might have harboured to disguise the

121

disturbing facts. The truth, and nothing but the truth, was the only way to retain his burgeoning affection in the girl's heart. He prayed silently that when she learnt about the whole sorry business her good judgement would not hold the sleazy details against him.

The last thing he wanted was to go down in this girl's estimation. An innate sixth sense told him he was falling in love. It was a sensation wildly remote and way beyond his experience – and one he had no desire to jeopardize. 'How's about you brew up a fresh pot of coffee?' he suggested warily, needing the time to organize his thoughts into the most persuasive order. 'And make it strong. This ain't gonna be the prettiest of stories.'

The sun was setting over the purple moulding of the Canyon rim when the account finally reached its conclusion with Deke's arrival in Glory Be. 'You know the rest.' It had been an earnest, heartfelt narration. The coffee pot was empty. Shadows were edging their way cautiously across the valley bottomland as the sun transformed into a ruby red platter. With worried eyes he surveyed the listeners, striving to read their thoughts. He was particularly anxious to gather Lucy's reaction. 'So what do you reckon? Have I passed the test?'

Nobody spoke. The atmosphere was tense. Ezra broke the impasse by getting himself upright and hobbling back into the cabin, where he procured a jug of moonshine. 'Reckon we could both do with a shot of something a heap stronger than coffee after that.' He poured them both a hefty slug. 'That was some tale. It sure was bad luck you not hearing about the surrender.'

Deke nodded, then turned his gaze to Lucy. It was her opinion he desperately wanted to hear. She came straight to the point. 'If'n that offer is still open, I can head into town once you've been to collect the stash, and then go pay off that scumbag.' Deke's whole body relaxed. He had passed muster. 'And I can't wait to see that slimeball's face when I hand it over.'

THIRTEEN

FATE PLAYS A WINNING HAND

At that very same moment, two riders were nudging their well lathered horses down the main street of Glory Be. They had ridden hard, pushing their mounts to the limit. The younger man brushed back a stray lock of yellow hair, his strikingly blue eyes ranging over the settlement. 'Let's hope this ain't gonna turn into a useless wild goose chase,' he commented to his buddy.

His stocky pard responded with a detached nod of the head. The lone eye adopted an equally judgemental view as he pulled out the well-thumbed news sheet, studying for the umpteenth time the penned depiction of the character responsible for their troubles. Neither man could ever have expected to be given this chance to square the score so soon after being ditched by their one-time commanding officer.

Lady Luck appeared to have dealt them a good hand after they reached Trinidad just over the border in Colorado territory. It was the wily Bone who figured out that Hogan would try to outfox them by avoiding No Man's Land. But the lady trickster could never be quite trusted to play her part honourably.

With barely two nickels to rub together between them, Charlie Bone had reluctantly been forced to sell his prized .50 calibre Remington Rolling Block rifle to a gun trader who had been admiring the weapon in the Segundo saloon.

'Reckon this is our lucky day, Charlie,' Blue declared, eyeing the wad of notes clutched tightly in his pard's fist. 'How's about you pass over a few of them greenbacks for me to win us a grubstake?' A flick of his head indicated the poker game being administered by a nattily clad dude who was clearly the house gambler.

Bone's good eye twitched. He was less than eager for his young sidekick to lose his dough at the tables – and Blue sensed the lack of enthusiasm. 'Come on, buddy. Ain't we dropped lucky in this burg? You got a good price for the rifle. And we're in this together now.' Rib-Eye was still not convinced. 'Just ten bucks. That's all I need, and I'll make that a hundred in no time. I can feel it in my blood!'

Never one to hold out for long when pressed, Bone reluctantly handed over the ten spot, much to his hot-headed pard's delight. Dusty wandered across to the table. 'Any chance of a good player joining this game?' he cockily enquired of the dealer.

Foxy Web Pickstave cast a nonchalant eye over the brash youngster. Straightaway he sensed easy prey. The waxed moustache twitched above a sly smirk. 'Reckon you've gotten the bottle to handle a proper game, kid?' he inquired, aiming a smug wink at the other two players.

The cutting jibe was not lost on the newcomer, but he managed to hold his quick temper in check. The sneering countenance was returned, along with a quiet promise as he leant forwards, slapping the dough on the table. 'You just deal the cards, jughead, and I'll rake in the dough.'

Without further ado he sat down, much to the relief of his watching associate. Bone then turned his attention to perusing a copy of the *San Isobel Courier* left on the bar by a customer. Only half an eye was imbibing the local news, the other carefully watching his partner.

The game made steady progress for the next half hour. And it certainly appeared as if the card angels were on Blue's side. Slowly he was amassing a sizeable pot, mainly at the expense of Foxy Web. The bandaged hand had certainly not hampered his luck with the pasteboards. The gambler was becoming ever more disgruntled. 'Seems to be my lucky day,' Blue piped up. A beaming smile made Pickstave even more fractious as the kid raked in another bunch of greenbacks. By this stage he must have been up by a hundred bucks.

There was only one way to deal with this irritating firebrand. Pickstave casually scratched his left ear. That was the house signal for two heavyweight guardians to move up behind the troublesome problem. It was now the kid's turn to deal the cards. Bets were placed and cards exchanged, followed by the usual cut and thrust associated with poker. By this time only the gambler and Blue were left in the game. Pickstave placed his bet, followed by the final call. Silence reigned supreme in the Segundo. All eyes were fastened on the young hotshot.

Blue slowly laid his hand down. 'Full house, queens on fours. Beat that, mister?' The ashen face gave him the answer he needed. 'Thought not. Guess I win again.' He reached out to claw in his winnings only to have a heavy hand slapped down preventing the move.

'Not so fast, kid. Where'd that Queen of Diamonds come from?'

Blue was nonplussed. 'What you getting at, buster?' he snapped.

'You're nothing but a cheating cardsharp,' Pickstave accused him, jumping to his feet. 'You already dealt me that lady from the pack. Grab him, boys.'

'Why, you conniving sidewinder,' Blue protested, pushing back his chair while reaching for his revolver. 'This is a blamed set-up.' But he never got the chance to draw. One of the minders slammed the barrel of his own gun across the kid's head.

At the same time the other tough jammed a

revolver in Rib-Eye's back. 'One false move and you're dead, fella,' he growled. 'We don't cotton to double-dealers in the Segundo. Now grab your pal and get out of town while you're still able.'

'What about the kid's winnings?' Rib-Eye complained.

'It's been confiscated. You have any objections, my friend here will show you the error of your ways.' The revolver traced a path down the old guy's stubble-coated face flicking the patch over his dead eye. 'Now git! And don't come back else I'll blow both your damned heads off.'

Charlie Bone had been adequately persuaded that departure was the best option for staying healthy. Watched by the angry gathering, he manhandled Dusty Blue outside and bundled the kid onto his horse. Blue was still groggy, unable to comprehend what had just occurred. Much to his pard's relief they were able to eat some trail dust before the kid realized what had happened.

'Hold up there, Charlie,' he objected reining to a halt. 'Those thieving turkeys robbed me of a rightful poke back there. I didn't need to cheat. The cards were on my side. I'm going back to show them nobody messes with Dusty Blue.'

'That ain't a good move, Dusty,' Bone countered. 'Two against that lot is bad odds. And anyway, we have a much more important appointment to keep.'

'What you burbling on about?'

'Take a look at this.' Rib-Eye handed over the news sheet jabbing a finger at the appropriate article, especially the pen drawing. 'Recognize him?' Charlie Bone had only spotted the vital report moments before the mayhem had blown up in the Segundo saloon.

Blue irritably snatched the paper from his outstretched hand casting a jaundiced eye over the selected missive. That was when his own peepers popped like champagne corks. All thoughts of evening the score with the felonious shysters in Trinidad were put on hold. This was far more important. 'According to this, Hogan has been one busy bee. A stage robbed and the passengers killed followed by a failed bank heist and another killing.' He emitted a grudging sigh of respect. 'Very busy indeed. I never figured the guy had it in him.'

'I can't believe the Major would engage in low-down stunts like those described here,' Bone contradicted. 'It just ain't his way.'

'You always were too darned trusting, Charlie.' Blue's caustic rejoinder poured scorn on his pard's opinion. 'It's down here in black and white. So why wouldn't it be true?' He didn't wait for a reply, instead spurring off again: 'We should get to this burg in four days if'n we push the nags. Don't forget there's twenty big ones at stake here, plus the reward for a dead or alive delivery. And I know which one I favour.' He chuckled uproariously much to his buddy's distaste. 'So let's ride. We don't want some other jaspers getting there afore us.'

Even the reluctant-to-condemn Bone was caught up in the chance to salvage their recent misfortunes for a life on Easy Street. 'And don't be forgetting the dough from that stage hold-up,' he enthused, his leathery features cracking into an aberrant half smile.

'Glad to see you're seeing sense at last, old buddy,' Blue declared. 'That guy made a big mistake taking us for a couple of mugs. Now he's gonna find out that was a real dumb move.'

The two unlikely partners made the journey south in three days, though both the men and their horses showed signs of the hurried journey.

'This sure is a good likeness,' Bone observed. 'Ain't no denying what you said about the Major having been hard at it since he abandoned us.'

Dusty Blue tossed a scornful look at his partner. 'You still can't shuck off that kowtowing can you, Rib-Eye? The moment that surrender was signed, he became just another washed-up soldier, no better than us.' His voice assumed a growled snarl of hatred. 'Worse, in fact, seeing as the skunk robbed us of our just desserts, then cast us afoot in the desert. Well, now we're gonna make him pay big time.'

'We don't know he's still hanging around here,' Bone objected. 'The guy could have skipped the territory.'

Blue scorned the notion. 'With his ugly mug staring out of papers and wanted posters in every town for two hundred miles around, my betting is he'll have gone to ground somewhere close. He's just waiting until the heat dies down before shipping out back east to play his good buddy act.' He spat in the dust. 'The only place he'll be going when I catch up with him is that graveyard back yonder.'

They pushed on down the street, eyes alert for the place mentioned in the article where any relevant information was to be delivered.

Nobody paid them any heed. Less than a week had passed since the grim upheaval that had shaken Glory Be to its very core. Yet already it was old news. The alleged killer had clearly slipped the net. The victims had been buried in the graveyard on the hill outside the town. And with bonuses no longer available, the townsfolk had reverted to their normal routines.

Only Elias Jacoby was still walking a tightrope of uncertainty. As long as that mysterious stranger remained at large, he could not settle. So far there had been no sighting of the varmint, even though his face had been splashed across the territory.

With Marshal Ike Stanford still lying abed in the surgery, acting lawman Sowbelly Clover had taken to his new role with gusto. He was lounging on the boardwalk in front of Windy Wilf's polishing his new badge when the two riders hove into view. Any strangers in Glory Be attracted attention, but these two were particularly worthy of note. He hustled into the gloomy interior of the saloon, striding across to the bar where Jacoby was carousing with Wilf Jenner.

'Hey boss!' Sowbelly was patently aware on which side his bread was buttered. 'Two trail bums have just arrived in town.'

Jacoby gave the news short shrift. 'So what?' he

snorted. 'Like all the others who've passed through here, they're likely heading for the gold strike at Cotopaxi.'

The acting marshal ignored the acerbic dig. 'You'll want to see these two, cos one of 'em's toting a copy of the *Courier*.'

FOURTEEN

THE DIE IS CAST

That news certainly perked up the slouching bank manager. Levering his bulky frame off the bar, Jacoby hustled across to the door. 'Could be they've recognized that killer,' Sowbelly added following close behind.

Jacoby eyed the two sorry specimens. They sure didn't have the look of hard-bitten gunfighters. That said, their mounts were well lathered, indicating they had been ridden hard. 'Check them out, Sowbelly. If'n they know something, get 'em up to the office. Me and Latigo will soon suss out whether they're time wasters.' He then left his underling, heading upstairs, his corpulent frame tingling with anticipation.

As expected, the newcomers pointed their horses towards the hitching rail outside the Segundo, where they dismounted and tied up. Clover came straight to the crux of the matter. 'Can you fellas identify the killer this town is after?' he snapped out barring their path. He nodded towards the paper clutched in Rib-Eye's hand. 'I'm figuring you ain't brought that rag to wipe your ass on.'

It was Dusty Blue who took the initiative. And he did not cotton to this guy's cocky manner. The pig farmer's regular fawning had been ditched since his recent rise in the pecking order. Although he had yet to be tested by any real law enforcement issue.

'Your name Jacoby?' Blue shot back running a jaundiced eye over this unkempt excuse for a lawman.

'This here authorizes me to check out any new-comers,' Sowbelly crowed, tapping the shiny badge. 'You can tell me anything you know and I'll see that it's passed on to *Mister* Jacoby.'

Blue's derisive look was intended to convey his contempt for the sneered retort. He pushed past Sowbelly, leaving him floundering, unsure how to react. 'What we have to say is for the organ grinder only,' he rasped. 'We don't deal with monkeys. Now out of my way.' Before Clover had recovered his com-posure, Blue, together with his more nervous associate, was inside the saloon. 'Where's the big shot who runs this place?' he shouted at Windy Wilf who was busy polishing glasses behind the bar.

Also caught napping by the kid's brusque mien, the saloon owner merely pointed to the stairs. 'I'll announce you boys,' Sowbelly jumped in, leading the way. 'Let's hope you have some good news so's I can catch up with this jasper and throw him in the hoosegow.'

Jacoby was all smiles when the tinstar made the introductions. He offered both men a drink, and a seat facing him across the huge oak desk. 'I assume that paper means you boys are acquainted with the guy plastered across the front page. The big question is. . . . Do you know where to find him?'

This was the question Blue had been expecting. And he had no intention of answering it. 'Ain't that reward a good enough reason? Besides, any other purpose we might have for running this critter down is our business.'

Jacoby's rubicund features hardened. 'You haven't answered my question. Where is the bastard now?'

'Yeah, mister. Let's be hearing something proper. We don't cotton to drifters after scrounging a grub-stake,' Latigo sneered attempting to regain his dented pride after being outmanoeuvred in the church. His hat barely concealed the bandage swathing his scalp. 'Could be you're just hoping to grab the reward money with some cock-and-bull story.'

'We can eyeball that fella. No doubt about that,' Rib-Eye butted in forcefully to ensure he was not sidelined. 'And you're right, we don't know his current whereabouts. But I can tell you straight, having known him for four years, he'll have gone to ground nearby. The Major is just waiting for the furore to die down before heading back east. Have you searched the town?'

'What do you take me for, buddy?' Jacoby ejaculated angrily. 'We've turned the place upside down. He ain't here. And I've had men guarding all the trails.'

'We didn't see nobody,' Bone observed. 'Seems like they all must have gotten bored and gone back home.'

Jacoby scowled, aiming a daggered look at his underling. Sowbelly blanched but remained silent. Blue butted in, assuming a more conciliatory attitude. 'In that case he must be hiding out someplace you haven't thought of. Or more likely, somebody is hiding him.'

Jacoby's haughty demeanour adopted a puzzled frown. He stroked his double chin thoughtfully. This was one notion he had not considered. 'Could be you're right there.' It was Sowbelly who then offered the crucial piece of unexpected knowledge.

'Now's I come to think about it,' he mused, 'When I visited the Courtright place the other day, Lucy was acting a mite shifty. I didn't give it much thought at the time. . . .' This regained the attention of all those present.

'Hurry it up, you old soak,' Latigo rasped impatiently, castigating the unlikely law officer. 'We ain't got all day.'

But Clover was not to be flustered. He had their attention and intended making the most of this new-found esteem. 'I noticed a lone saddled horse tied up outside the barn. It couldn't have been old Ezra's, seeing as he's still waiting on that new pegleg. And

136

there were three mugs on the table. When I asked her how she was going to manage the spread with her pa out of action, she mumbled something about having taken on a hired hand. But then she quickly changed it to something she would be doing soon.'

'Why didn't you mention this before?' Jacoby rapped.

The pig farmer shrugged. 'It didn't seem important at the time.' It was a somewhat lame excuse. Acting Marshal Clover now grasped that a clued-up lawman would have been looking out for any strange occurrences and questioning them. The enormity of the task he had willingly undertaken was now laid bare. Maybe he had taken on too much.

Not one to cry over split milk, Jacoby knew that fast action was needed to rectify the omission. 'I'll deal with you later,' he snorted fastening his attention wholly on to this pair of drifters. There was clearly more to them than he had initially thought. 'I take it you know how to handle those hoglegs strapped to your legs?' A sceptical glower fastened on to the kid. 'That bandaged hand looks to be an impediment, from where I'm sitting.'

Blue gave the view a caustic snort of derision. Then without further ado he drew his pistol and twirled it around his middle finger, tossing it into the air before catching it with a flourish. 'That answer your question?' he smirked, arrogance oozing from every pore of his cocksure demeanour. 'Don't be thinking the loss of a measly little finger will spoil my aim. And the other mitt is just as deadly.' He then performed the same stunt left-handed.

'Very impressive,' Jacoby sighed, not in the least taken in by the showground flummery, 'if'n you wanted a job as a juggler, that is. I only employ guys who are prepared to use those shooters in a real situation.'

'My partner here is just showing off, Mister Jacoby,' Bone said pinning the kid down with a derogatory look of vexation. Instead he adopted a far more pragmatic stance. 'He lost that finger when a rattler bit him. I had to chop it off.' Without the slightest hesitation he hurried on. 'And we weren't just bystanders in the recent conflict. Riding with the Rebel Raiders needed grit and resilience to survive for as long as we did.'

'The Rebel Raiders!' The infamous name certainly grabbed the cunning businessman's interest. It even made an impression on Latigo. 'Why didn't you boys say so before? I could sure use a couple of devil-may-care gunnies with a rep like your'n. What handle does this mystery killer go under?'

'Does the name Deke Hogan ring a bell?' Bone declared proudly.

Gaping mouths answered his question. The Rebel Raiders led by that infamous guerrilla leader had been prime targets for the Union forces. Capturing him now would be something to enhance Elias Jacoby's reputation and standing in the territory.

Latigo was less enthusiastic. Guys like these two could become a threat to his own position in the hierarchy. They would need to be watched like hawks. His boss paid no heed to the bodyguard's lukewarm acceptance of his proposition. 'It was Hogan who caused all the trouble round here. He killed a top gun hand called Nevada Bass Tiptree. Ever heard of him?'

Blue responded with a listless shrug. 'It don't mean nothing to me,' he said still smarting from his buddy's gibe in respect of his gun-spinning caper. 'All I'm bothered about is getting even with the skunk that did the dirty on us.'

'That's what I like to hear. You boys could do a lot worse than working for me. And I pay good money,' Jacoby continued. 'So what do you say?'

Blue answered for them both, not bothering to consult his less than eager partner. 'You've gotten yourself a deal, boss. When do we start?'

Jacoby sealed the understanding by topping up their glasses. 'Let's drink to a fruitful relationship and the removal of a thorn in my flesh. 'Cos after what you've told me, I have reason to believe our mutual adversary might well be hiding out on a horse ranch not far from here.'

He went on to reveal what he expected from their first job. And it concerned the forthcoming eviction of the Courtrights from Lodge Pole Canyon. Jacoby had decided that a week was too long to wait. He wanted them removed forthwith. And these two had arrived at just the right time to bring it into effect. After explaining the circumstances, he finished with a promise that saw Dusty Blue's eyes lighting up. 'And there will be a substantial bonus for each of you when the job is done.'

Jacoby peeled off a wad of bills from a hefty poke and handed the dough to Blue. 'Get yourself some new duds and a bath. I don't employ trail bums. Then go see Doc Barnett and get that finger seen to. When you're fixed up, report to Latigo here. He's my second-in-command and will give you directions of how to get there.'

After the duo had departed Latigo voiced his scepticism. 'I don't trust those two boobies. They could be in league with the guy we're after.'

'Don't reckon so,' Jacoby countered. 'The anger they displayed against that guy was no piece of theatre. They want him as dead as we do. Particularly the kid.'

'Do you want for me to tag along and make sure they don't make a kibosh of the whole thing?'

A shake of the head was Jacoby's response. 'If'n that guy is hiding out in the Canyon and cuts up rough, it ain't our responsibility. We can say that those two have been acting on their own. The *Courier* will prove that.' The banker hooked his thumbs into his vest pockets while watching the two oblivious newcomers cross the street and enter the barber's shop.

'But then we'll know exactly where to find our illusive will-o'-the-wisp. There's plenty of folks in town willing to form an official posse. And they'll be more than happy to arrest the Courtrights as accessories to murder when they know this bad boy has been hiding out in Lodge Pole Canyon. We'll be in the clear again, and that land will be confiscated as the proceeds of a criminal deception. Whatever happens, we come out as winners.'

'What if'n this Hogan ain't down there?' Windy Wilf had posed the question also looming in Latigo's head. 'What happens then?'

Jacoby shook his head. 'Should he have skipped the territory, that article and the drawing are bound to attract other bounty hunters like moths to a flame. He won't get far. You boys should look to the bigger picture, like me.' He drew on his cigar, puffing out a plume of satisfied smoke.

FIFTEEN

PLAYING CATCH-UP

Dusty Blue and his partner had camped out in a shallow depression overlooking the Courtright spread. His finger still hurt after being stitched up. But rather than hinder him, it made Blue all the more determined to exact his revenge. And the special glove he had been given sure helped. They were up at first light keeping a sharp eye on the place for any sign of movement.

The sun had barely raised its head above the eastern rim of the canyon when a solitary figure emerged from the barn riding a horse. Both men were instantly on the alert. 'That's him,' Bone hissed, his single eye glinting in the weak sunlight. The loss of his other had certainly not impaired the guy's overall vision. 'I'd recognize that straight-backed gait any place. It's just like we figured. He's been hiding out down there. For some reason the owner must have offered him a refuge until the heat dies down.'

'More like he's bribed the jasper with a wedge of our dough,' Blue snarled, curling his lip with disdain.

'So where in tarnation do you reckon he's going at such an early hour?'

'Obvious, ain't it?' Blue rasped, grinding his teeth. 'The rat must have stashed the bank money and is going to collect it before making a run for the border. Well, he ain't gonna reach it. Get your horse buddy, we'll follow him and see where the skunk leads us. Then it's goodbye to you Major Deke Hogan, and hello Easy Street for us.'

The fired-up tearaway failed to note the uncertain, doubtful consequence his blunt threat had engendered in his partner. Disappointment rather than fixated revenge were his main spurs for sticking with Dusty Blue in their journey towards a finale. All the same, Charlie Bone was just as eager to catch up with their one-time leader. Being an impoverished drifter did not sit well with him any more than it did his associate. He just hoped that a satisfactory agreement could be reached without any blood being spilled.

It was mid-morning before Hogan drew his mount to a halt below a towering pinnacle of rock. There he ground hitched the animal and climbed up a bank of loose scree to the foot of the prominent edifice known as Bodkin Butte. The two pursuers similarly paused behind some rocks, watching their quarry as he scrabbled around at the base of the rock face.

'What did I tell you?' Blue muttered angrily. 'He must have hidden the dough up there.' Both men stayed hidden as they observed the sack of greenbacks being extracted from beneath a boulder.

Totally unaware he was under surveillance, Hogan slithered back down the slope, fully intent on making a return to the homestead to present Lucy Courtright with the sum needed to clear her loan agreement with the Land Agency. What he intended doing beyond that was still undecided. Much as he wanted to stick around in the company of such a delightful employer, his conscience was egging him to head back to Missouri, at least until he made sure his family was settled into the new order the country had delivered following the surrender.

He had fastened the sack to his pommel horn and was about to mount up when a voice from the recent past jerked him out of his reverie.

'Stay right where you are, Judas.' Blue's curt order found the recipient frozen to the spot. 'Figuring you could outrun your old pals was a dumb move . . . *Major*!' The word was chock full of derision. 'Now it's payback time. Only difference is, in this share out there's only two winners. Me and Rib-Eye here. Unless of course you count the coyotes. The loser earns himself a bullet and an unexpected meal for the scavengers.' He laughed heartily at this piece of witty jousting. But there was no humour in the cold mockery.

Hogan was genuinely shocked by this sudden

arrival of his old partners. Momentarily stunned into silence he soon found his voice. 'How in thunder did you track me down?' he enquired. 'I didn't leave any clues. Lady Lucky must have been shining on you.'

'Luck wasn't in it. Show him Charlie.' Bone tossed his copy of the *San Isobel Courier* at the feet of his old boss. The penned depiction stared up at him. 'We came across this while passing through Trinidad. And there's a two thousand reward for your capture been given by a fat cat called Jacoby in Glory Be. He's awful keen to see you buried six feet under. And we intend to grant his wish and collect at the same time. Ain't that so, Charlie?' He didn't wait for a reply. His finger tightened on the trigger. 'Say your prayers. But make it short and sweet.'

'I can't let you do it, Dusty.' Now it was Blue's turn to freeze. The double click from behind was no rattler's warning. But it was a stipulation nonetheless from a direction he had not anticipated. 'I'm sure we can come to an arrangement that suits us all. No need for any gunplay.' Bone's suggestion was almost a supplication. 'I don't want to pull this trigger but I will if'n you don't see sense.'

'Why, you double-dealing sonofabitch.' Anger at having been duped caused a pall of red mist to slide down, blotting out any rational thought the kid might have entertained. The old fart must have read his mind regarding the share out of the dough, or lack of in his case. His whole being was now focused on obliterating the threat to his plan.

Half turning, he swung the .36 Navy Colt round

intending to catch his double-crossing pard on the blind side. But the wily Rib-Eye had anticipated such a manoeuvre and had secreted himself behind a Joshua tree. Others had figured to pull the same stunt before. Not being a fast draw artiste, the older man had perfected his ruse to good effect. Blue managed to trigger off a single shot before he was struck down by two well placed bullets straight to the heart. The kid was dead before he hit the ground.

'Best not try to pull a similar stunt, Major,' the crafty veteran advised holding his gun rock steady. 'You know I ain't a-feared to protect myself. And you should also understand that unlike our old pal here, I had no intention of running off with the whole caboodle.'

'Glad to hear it, Charlie,' Hogan replied shaking his head. One second he was aiming to head back to the ranch and to complete his benevolent gesture, the next all hell breaks loose around him. 'This is like being back in the thick of the action when Axton's Cavalry ambushed us in the Ozark Breaks.'

Charlie cackled to himself. 'I was thinking along the same lines myself. Now turn around slow and easy. My trigger finger's kinda twitchy, and I'd hate to send you down the same road as poor old Blue.'

Hogan likewise was well aware of his old buddy's casual yet ruthless streak, and kept his hands raised. Face to face, he was surprised to see that Bone had holstered his revolver and was perched on a rock rolling a stogie, which he lit up and handed to his old boss.

'The kid had it coming. I knew he had no intention of splitting the take with me. And I know you'll play fair whatever your decision might be regarding its disposal.' He arrowed a searching look at Hogan. 'Am I right in thinking that?'

'I don't want to lie to you, Charlie. You deserve better.' He signalled for his associate to mount up.

On the way back to Lodge Pole Canyon, Hogan expressed his regret at leaving Rib-Eye Charlie stranded following the Tucumcari hold-up then brought him up-to-date with his dubious adventures so far. The older man was all ears.

'So you see,' he explained hoping the older man would go along with his plan. 'I have promised to help the girl and her pa out. Then I'm heading back east. I'd like for you to accompany me. That dough will help our kinfolks during the upheaval the War's left behind.'

He paused to allow his objective for the distribution of the money to sink in before adding a sweetener. 'But don't think my good-buddy mission is going to leave us empty-handed. We're as much charity cases as anybody else, ain't we?' He winked at the old veteran, whose attempted response left them both chortling uproariously.

'You sure don't do things by halves, Major,' he remarked with a mixed degree of respect and awe. 'And it don't look like things are over yet.'

'You're right there, buddy,' Hogan sighed. 'I'm stumped as to how I can force Jacoby into admitting his role in the stagecoach robbery and death of his

147

partner Howard Kemper. It's a conundrum that's been taxing my brain ever since being accused of both crimes. The only proof I have regarding the identity of the stage robber is this.' He pulled out the silver concho with its distinctive Indian symbols.

His associate's piercing gaze studied the shiny chunk of metal. 'That's a Comanche emblem. And I've seen it recently in Jacoby's office.' His leathery face creased up in a lurid grin. 'A hardcase employed by the guy was wearing a black leather vest lined with these beauties. And one was missing. I didn't give it any thought at the time. But this must be the missing concho.'

Hogan's face lit up. 'That's all I need to prove it was Latigo who robbed that stage and killed the passengers because they must have recognized him. And that makes Jacoby an accessory.' He clapped his pal on the back. 'Looks like I'm in the clear, pal, thanks to you.'

After returning to the ranch, Hogan introduced his old associate and handed over the three thousand, much to the gratitude of Lucy Courtright who burst into tears. 'I don't know how to thank you,' she sobbed. 'We'll make sure to pay you back once the spread is working properly, won't we, Pa?'

'Sure will,' Ezra proclaimed stomping about on his new leg. 'That skunk Jacoby is in for one heck of a surprise when he discovers he can't ride rough shod over folks. I can't wait to see his face when we give him the dough.'

SIXTEEN

PAYBACK TIME

Over a much needed pot of strong coffee and some delicious homemade cookies, a plan was worked out how to trap Elias Jacoby into divulging his part in the wickedly shameful felonies that had plagued Glory Be in recent months. With Ezra and his daughter driving the wagon, Hogan and his pal followed behind. Only when they were approaching the outskirts of the town did Hogan conceal himself under a tarpaulin. It was a case of déjà vu in reverse. But on this occasion he was not fleeing for his life.

Muted voices penetrated the heavy cover as passers-by hailed the Courtrights. 'Good to see you up and about, Ezra,' could be heard issuing from numerous throats. 'All you need now is a parrot on your shoulder and we can call you Long John,' one wag joked, much to the delight of all concerned, including Ezra Courtright. They were a popular

149

family. Hogan had no doubts that Lucy could persuade enough people to back her claim that Deke Hogan was an innocent victim.

Ezra steered the wagon round to the rear of the saddle shop. On being given the signal that nobody was around, Hogan slipped from cover, scuttling through the open trap door down into the cellar. Upstairs he outlined his plan. His first request was to Ezra. 'If'n you could accompany me to the marshal's office and get him to back up my claim against Jacoby we could all hide in the back room of the bank while Lucy makes her entrance at the front.'

The old bronc buster was all for it. 'I'll have Doc Barnett and Harvey Bookbinder come along as well. They'll be mighty eager to hear what Jacoby has to say when you confront the crook.'

'Keep out of sight until I've gotten the drop on him,' Hogan warned. 'I don't want anyone else getting hurt. If'n they decide to cut up rough, leave the heavy stuff to me and Rib-Eye.'

Once the essence of the trap had been agreed upon, Lucy accompanied the two war veterans along to the law office, her father hobbling along behind using a crutch. She was on tenterhooks. This scheme to ensnare Elias Jacoby depended on them being able to persuade a crotchety old rooster like Sowbelly Clover to believe their assertion.

She need not have worried. After listening intently to the cogent arguments put forth in support of Hogan's innocence, Sowbelly left the jailhouse. The surprisingly agile pig farmer hustled along to the

Paradise saloon where his pals were sat in their usual place chewing the cud. What he had to relate must have struck the right note. The medic and his pal the undertaker soon returned with the acting marshal to the jail.

'Is this true, Ezra?' Doc Barnett asked the homesteader, who was waiting anxiously outside. 'Have you been harbouring this man?'

'It sure is, and he ain't no killer nor a robber. We have proof that Jacoby was behind it and Latigo Rennick pulled the job.' He gestured for the two respected worthies to meet the man himself.

They all trooped into the jail where Hogan was waiting. 'So this is the man we're supposed to believe just stumbled into this mess by accident.' Always the more questioning of the group, Bookbinder's assertion was laced with scepticism. 'It's a hard claim to swallow.'

'It's true,' Lucy affirmed with vigour. 'I was unsure when he sought refuge in the store. But I'm certain now that he has been wrongly accused by the true culprit. It's not just his word I'm accepting. He has given me the money to pay off our bank loan in full. Money he was taking back east to help rebuild the South after the War.' Lucy was careful not to mention the manner in which that money had been acquired. Luckily, the men were too stunned to enquire.

Thankfully, Lucy's fervent defence of the much vilified stranger appeared to satisfy the deputation, who agreed to act as vital witnesses at the forthcoming

151

exposure. Hogan quickly filled them in on his plan of action.

At this time of day, it was confirmed that Elias Jacoby would most likely be in his office at the bank – that very same one where Hogan had first sought refuge. Fortunately it was on the same side of the street as the saddle store.

So while Lucy openly strolled down the boardwalk clutching her valuable payment, Hogan and his entourage sneaked along behind the frontage, entering the rear of the bank with a key held by the law office in case of emergencies. It was a stipulation the council had insisted upon, much to Jacoby's annoyance. And this was adjudged to be a crisis situation.

'Absolute silence when we get inside,' Hogan insisted. 'If'n he suspects a thing, all hell could break loose. Let me and Rib-Eye carry the can.' Once inside, they listened intently for the arrival of Lucy Courtright.

A knock on the door leading into the bank area saw Jacoby reply with his customary haughty command. 'Come in! What is it, Simkins? I'm busy at the moment. Can't it wait?'

'Miss Courtright is here to see you, sir,' was the timid reply. 'She says that you are expecting her.'

'Is she now!' The crooked banker's officious manner changed instantly to one of wary curiosity. He threw a puzzled look towards Latigo. 'Show her in immediately.'

Lucy flounced into the room and slapped the packet of money on the desk. Then without uttering a word, she extracted the signed contract from her coat pocket and dropped it next to the money. 'It's all there,' she proclaimed breezily. 'Now if you would be good enough to sign off the loan, I will leave you and your erm . . . associate. . . .' Her nose wrinkled as if a bad smell had entered the room before retrieving the signed paper '. . . to plan more underhanded trickery.' And with that snappy riposte she departed, leaving Jacoby and the bank guard dumbfounded.

The corrupt banker snatched up the packet and tore it open. Bundles of dollar bills stared back at him. It was the hardcase who found his voice first. 'Where in blue blazes did she find that kind of dough?'

The rear door of the office was silently pushed open. Unseen by the two brigands who were staring open mouthed at the money, Hogan stepped into the room. He flipped the silver concho into the air watching it arc silently, the carved depiction catching the sunlight beaming in through a window. Then it clanged on the desk rolling across and coming to rest face up beside its owner. Latigo was flummoxed. A reflexive reaction found his hand reaching for the gap in his vest from where the lost item had been torn.

'Guess you must have been wondering where you lost that,' Hogan announced locking eyes on the startled killer. 'Well, I found it clutched in the hand of the lady you murdered after that stagecoach robbery.' The frosty grin failed to reach his eyes, which remained fixed on his adversary. 'It was this fat

153

slob who planned the heist and you that carried it out.'

Latigo's crusty features broke in a twisty sneer. There was no point in denying it. 'The stupid dame oughtn't to have grabbed hold of my bandanna. I had to kill her when she eyeballed me. But you'll never prove a thing.'

'The killings were all a mistake,' Jacoby interjected, sweat dribbling down his blotched cheeks. He took hold of the bundle of greenbacks. 'Here take it. And there's more in the safe. All you have to do is forget you ever heard of Glory Be. Just disappear and I'll place a report in the *Courier* to say it was all a big mistake.'

Hogan ignored the pleading attempt at bribery. 'And then there was your partner whom you shot in cold blood, right where I'm standing now.'

'That wasn't me,' Jacoby whined, pointing an accusatory finger at his underling. 'He killed Howard.'

Latigo snarled, unwilling to accept all the blame. 'And then you put the blame on this guy, not to mention planning the whole caper.'

'You fellas heard enough out there?' Hogan called to those listening in.

'We sure have, Mr Hogan,' Sowbelly declared stepping into the room, accompanied by his sidekicks. He was holding an old rust-pitted .36 Navy Colt in his hand that had clearly seen better days. 'You two scumbags are under arrest for robbery and murder!' The stand-in lawman was taking his responsibilities seriously. Behind him, Doc Barnett and the undertaker hovered, still in shock regarding these sudden and unsettling revelations.

Of the two miscreants Latigo had no intention of submitting to this grizzled has-been. He hawked out a mirthless guffaw. 'Looks like this is a meeting of the Old Timers' Committee. Well, I ain't sticking around to take part.' And without any further comment, he pushed Jacoby into the lawman. Clover in turn stumbled back into his buddies. The sudden retaliation had caught them all on the hop. Even Hogan was taken by surprise. Unable to respond with the floundering group blocking his aim, he was left struggling to retain his own balance.

Latigo took advantage of the disorder by grabbing the money bag. A couple of shells were pumped at his adversary as the brigand hauled open the door to the front office. The shots missed Hogan, but one struck Rib-Eye in the chest, further adding to the mayhem. Desperation gripped the fugitive, who had no intention of shaking hands with the hangman.

He slammed the office door shut, turning the key in the lock to delay any pursuit. The smoking revolver effectively doused any threat of retaliation by the tellers. The gunshots in the inner sanctum had precipitated a dive of all parties on to the floor. Simpkins was the only one who attempted any sort of resistance. He soon retired beneath the counter when another bullet ploughed into the woodwork inches from his head.

'Anybody else tries to act the hero, they'll be

stoking up the fires of hell,' Latigo rasped lunging across to the front door.

Out on the street, the owlhoot leapt on to his horse and galloped off. Lucy was striding back to the saddle store when she heard the outburst. Turning around, she spotted the killer emerging from the bank clutching the bag. 'Stop that man!' she called out. 'He's just robbed the bank.'

But the bleak winds of destiny had driven everybody indoors. Dust devils collided with one another in the middle of the street, frolicking in a fiendish dance of abandonment. Clumps of tumbleweed followed close behind, hoping to join in the ghoulish festivities. The sunlight had faded to a dull ochre in the haze of sand being whipped up. Just another spring day in Glory Be.

But this one was anything but normal. Lucy dashed back into the bank where the terrified occupants were slowly emerging from their panic-stricken trauma. In the back office she found the medic bending over the injured war veteran. She gasped aloud as Doc Barnett shook his head. 'Sorry Mr Hogan. I'm afraid your pal is dead.'

Hogan swallowed, holding back a cry of anguish. But this was no time for histrionics. Anxious to redress the gunman's reversal of what had begun as a clear-cut thwarting of Elias Jacoby's criminal ambitions, Deke urgently began issuing orders. 'Make sure this varmint is locked up tight, marshal,' he declared with a growl of abhorrence. His manhandling of the sweating villain was accompanied by a couple of hefty smacks that left the skunk dazed and bloodied. Nobody sought to stop him. 'I'm going after that killer and I ain't coming back without him.'

Lucy had quickly absorbed the grim scenario. 'I saw Rennick heading south towards Wagon Wheel Gap and the New Mexico border. But be careful,' she urged. 'That skunk is slippery as a wet fish. And the sandstorm will give him an edge.'

Hogan nodded his thanks, giving her a quick peck on the cheek. There was no time for any further endearment. Outside, the storm had increased in ferocity, forcing him to tie down his hat. He leapt on to a horse that obviously belonged to Jacoby. He wouldn't need it anymore. Narrowing his eyes to thin slivers, he pointed the animal south.

Once the town limits were left behind, all Hogan could do was pray he was following the right trail. The killer might well have decided to lie up some place and ambush him, or he could easily have struck across country and so might be anywhere by now. On the other hand, nobody would leave a well used road under these harsh conditions. He carried on, steadily gaining height. Rougher under foot, the trail narrowed as it snaked ever higher. But at the same time visibility was improving, the wind noticeably slackening pace.

On cresting the next rise, an iridescent vista emerged from the gloom. Full clarity had been restored. The trail became a loose path through the rocky outcrops encompassing Wagon Wheel Gap. But crucially, there was his quarry, no more than half

157

a mile ahead. All of Hogan's senses prickled with anticipation. He spurred on the black stallion, urging it into a gallop.

Latigo must have sensed his presence. He looked behind, disturbed to see his pursuer rapidly gaining ground. Jacoby's black was a far more resilient mount than his own mustang, and the gap between them was quickly narrowing. The outlaw cursed for not having commandeered the prize Arab stallion. Too late for any regrets now. But the error made him realize there could be no outrunning his tail.

There was only one option left for the frantic desperado. He hauled rein, dismounted and stood in the middle of the trail, awaiting the arrival of his adversary. This was to be a classic showdown, and only one of them would walk away.

As Hogan drew closer he knew what the gunman sought. A winner-takes-all contest to the finish. Without taking his eyes off the guy, he drew to a halt some fifty yards short of the lone figure. Before advancing to meet him, he checked his Remington. This kind of showdown was rare. Only a couple of times in his military career had he taken part in such a duel. On both occasions he had obviously lived to fight another day.

'That's far enough, mister,' Latigo called out when his opponent was twenty feet distant. 'The name's Latigo Rennick,' he said. 'You may have heard of me.'

'I seem to recall you're worth a good reward – dead only!' Hogan goaded the other man. 'I aim to collect. A rat that guns down women and children don't deserve a good hanging.'

It had the desired effect. Latigo bristled angrily. 'She brought it on herself. I had no choice.'

'There's always a choice, mister,' Hogan hissed. 'And you chose the wrong one. Me happening along offered you and that weasel back yonder an easy target to hang the blame on. Bad move. Just like it was a bad move figuring you could take me down out here. Now you're gonna pay the price.'

'We'll see about that.' Latigo was in no way intimidated by Hogan's brusque mien. 'Delivering up the body of a notorious guerrilla raider will enhance my rep.'

Hogan laughed. 'Other fellas have tried and failed.' He hunkered down ready for the draw. 'Let's just get this over with.' He pulled out a pocket watch and set it on a rock. 'When the music stops playing, we do the business. Agreed?'

A sneered grin was the only reply. Hogan flipped the lid and a mellifluous jingle resonated across the bleak expanse of Wagon Wheel Gap. Filling the static air with its haunting refrain, the fateful music slowly wound down. He was studying his opponent for that significant moment. On the two previous occasions he had used this ploy, his sly adversaries had sought an advantage by drawing early. Would Latigo pull a similar trick? It seemed likely.

Slowly and more slowly the melodic aria trundled onwards to its end – until the critical point when Latigo sprang into action. His hand clawed at the pistol butt. Sunlight slanted off the shimmering metal as the gun rose, the hammer racking back as he squeezed the trigger. But that was it. A bullet struck him high in the chest, a second caught him in the throat. The failed gunslinger threw his arms wide, tottering back. Blood-red eyes glazed over, a perfect match for the pulsating flow spurting from his fatal injuries. Life and all its earthly trimmings rapidly slipped away.

The winning gladiator ambled over to his victim. 'A cheat always collects his just desserts,' he said blowing the smoke from his pistol barrel. 'Tell that to Old Nick when he calls you out.' He then heaved the body up on to the waiting mustang and tied it down securely.

Deke Hogan's mind was full of mixed emotions on the ride back to Glory Be. Pleasant thoughts regarding plans for an idyllic life with the girl of his dreams could not replace the heartache of losing a valued ally. Old Rib-Eye had momentarily strayed from a righteous path tempted by the covetous God of Easy Money.

There was also the lingering question that at some point he would have to return to Missouri. But for the moment that could be left on the back burner.

Everything in God's own time. As for the immediate future, Lucy Courtright's beautiful countenance held centre stage. All else had been pushed to one side.